THE NORDIC TRANSLATION SERIES

SPONSORED BY THE NORDIC COUNCIL
OF THE GOVERNMENTS OF DENMARK, FINLAND,
ICELAND, NORWAY, AND SWEDEN
ADVISORY COMMITTEE:
EINAR I. HAUGEN, HARALD S. NAESS, AND
RICHARD B. VOWLES, CHAIRMAN

Bread of Love

THE UNIVERSITY

OF WISCONSIN PRESS

MADISON AND

MILWAUKEE 1965

PEDER SJÖGREN

Bread of Love

KÄRLEKENS BRÖD

TRANSLATED FROM THE SWEDISH

BY RICHARD B. VOWLES

Published by the University of Wisconsin Press
Madison and Milwaukee
P.O. Box 1379, Madison, Wisconsin 53701

English translation copyright © 1965 by the
Regents of the University of Wisconsin

Originally published by
Medéns Förlags Aktiebolag
Stockholm, Sweden
Copyright © 1945 by Medéns Förlags Aktiebolag

Printed in the United States of America by
North Central Publishing Co., St. Paul, Minnesota

Library of Congress Catalog
Card Number 65-24189

CONTENTS

INTRODUCTION

A recurrent theme is probably as good a clue as any to an author's essential art, and so it is with the contemporary Swedish writer of fiction, Peder Sjögren.

In his first novel, *Black Palms*, an aged Estonian woman reminisces about the time she made a pilgrimage, as a young girl, in order to catch a glimpse of the Tsar. Just at the fleeting, precious moment of her dreams, a boozing reprobate of a man playfully approaches from behind and puts his dirty hands over her eyes in a "guess who" gesture, thus denying her the long-anticipated pleasure. In one of his latest radio plays, "Nobel Festival," adapted from the short story "The Quarry," Sjögren returns to the theme. This time a retired workman from northern Sweden makes a pilgrimage to Stockholm to see a Nobel Prize winner arrive at the central railroad station, and his brief, precious vision is denied in exactly the same fashion. In both cases the offender seeks to repair the damage but succeeds only in compounding it.

Three observations should be made. First, Sjögren is fascinated with the simple innocents of life who are steadily frustrated and thwarted by the forces of evil, an evil only occasionally aware of its own identity. Secondly, he exacts such a powerful irony from the intersection of these converging elements that the idea of irony tends to become a major preoccupation in his narrative art. Thirdly, he is a great manipulator. At best, he, the storyteller, merges with fate itself; at worst, he indulges himself in a kind of fantastic puppetry that is worth watching even when we are all too conscious of the complex of strings. It is tempting to describe Sjögren as a proletarian Isak Dinesen, but the comparison creates more problems than it solves. First a proper introduction should be performed.

Gösta Tage Filip Sjögren was born in 1905, outside of Växjö, in the province of Småland, an area of Sweden already familiar to readers of Vilhelm Moberg and Pär Lagerkvist. He came from a family of farmers and factory managers in the sawmills and glass factories particular to that region. At the age of ten he was moved to Stockholm to continue his schooling. Sjögren's father hoped to interest him in politics, but his interests then ran to art and especially to cubist experiment. At the age of seventeen he was packed off to Rome with parental blessing, and this move was the beginning of a peripatetic, adventurous life that led him to the Balkans, Spain, North Africa, Poland, and Finland. Today, Sjögren has had enough of travel. His time is fully devoted to craft, whether it is carpentry or writing, either in his winter quarters in Bromma, a western suburb of Stockholm, or in a summer cottage which he built himself in Svinesund, near the Norwegian border — a part of Sweden which particularly pleases him because it combines the Småländsk landscape of his origin with the west coast physiognomy around Göteborg, his wife's home.

Sjögren first attracted attention as a journalist who was able to combine a colorful reportage for the Stockholm daily, *Dagens Nyheter*, with chicken farming in Spain. During the Spanish Civil War he joined the Loyalist side and was wounded in combat. After his recovery, he was arrested as a spy suspect, but subsequently escaped from Spain on a British man-of-war. His best articles, which he himself illustrated with bold brush drawings, were collected in *Bar Barbar* (1937), whose title is a jesting reference to a wine depot where Scandinavian seamen, cleaned of everything but their trousers, could come for a slug of wine and a sheet-metal roof over their heads. His subjects are the Spanish character, the church, bullfighting — at which he tried his hand — and, of course, the war itself. "This isn't Spain, with its famous sun," Sjögren wrote in the Preface; "this reportage is from a country in the shadows. Pieces of a country in the shadows."

In spite of this book and occasional radio plays and short stories, Sjögren did not attract attention until the appearance of *Black Palms* (*Svarta palmkronor*, 1944), which has since gone into several editions and obviously become his most popular book. In some ways it is a continuation of *Bar Barbar* that has assumed the shape of a novel. Here Sjögren concentrates on his Scandinavian deserter seamen leading their beachcombing existence on the Graos waterfront, Valencia's harbor. There is Papilla, a young Finnish girl, quick and silent like a lizard, a fascinating confection of innocence and experience. She feels obliged to give her love to the drunken Colette, who saved her life at sea, but she is really drawn to the albino-blond Olofson, a shy giant of a man who is the ringleader of the harbor bums. There is a bordello madam who reads novels voraciously and an anarchistic flute player, and other assorted gypsies, pickpockets, nuns, whores, and policemen. The villain of the piece is Lassen, the pastor of the seamen's home and a masterly portrayal of hypocrisy. He indulges his lusts and continually threatens the seamen with the arrival of the "Black Ship" which will take them back to a life of responsibility. The book seethes with life and fantasy, one must admit, whether or not the hymn to a rummy innocence is palatable or not.

Is it a song of praise to the Spanish people? "No, not at all," says Sjögren.

It's an attempt to regulate the concept of good and evil, morality and immorality. Those of us, chiefly of the church, who are stamped as sinners, sometimes stand — yes, perhaps always stand — significantly nearer God than the moralists themselves. Christendom is one thing; "priestdom" is another. During my six-year stay in Spain I saw Catholicism at close hand. I know that the Civil War, which I took part in, at bottom was a battle between the church and mankind, between mendacity and truth. The aim of my book is very serious, but the means are playful — one might even say frolicsome.

If Sjögren's life at this point resembled Hemingway's, his first novel suggested to most reviewers a comparison with John Steinbeck's *Tortilla Flat*. Sjögren was not so much irritated by what he took to be allegations of plagiarism, but annoyed that he had made so little impression as a journalist.

Until the novel appeared, I believed, in my naïveté, that I was somewhat respected and read as a columnist. But after that, I could assume it no longer. It so happens that all the scenes, figures, and milieux that appear here had already been published as I experienced them (almost in the fashion of a diary). These pieces had appeared in the chief Swedish newspapers over a space of about ten years, from my 25th to my 35th year . . . but when the book appeared, not a critic (least of all those for the newspapers in which I was published) failed to mention that I had plagiarized Steinbeck's *Tortilla Flat*. Nobody had read my modest little reports in the press, or at least remembered them.

Whatever the similarities, no one could call in question Sjögren's fresh and vigorous originality.

A pacificist, Peder Sjögren has fought in two wars. His second novel, *Bread of Love* (*Kärlekens bröd*, 1945), is based on his experiences as a volunteer in the Finnish Continuation War of 1941–44. The speaker of the entire story is a soldier who has the task of reporting to a mother the deaths of her two sons, both destined to failure, one incapable of positive identity and the other in flight from himself in a desperation to do and be. The novel probes to the very root of character and maintains a particular tension by the device of confrontation between the soldier narrator and the mother at a moment of unusual stress.

One would hardly expect Sjögren's taste for the exotic to thrive outside a semitropical milieu, but such was the horror of the Finno-Russian War and such is Sjögren's sharp reportorial pen which, in fact, transcends the reportorial through its brilliance of imagery, that a frozen fantasy on the edge of dream is the result, perhaps the kind of vision one has on the brink of death by exposure to cold. Many details are memorable: the animated sculpture of corpses frozen into grotesque positions, stalagmites of urine, bicycles melted into an indistinguishable mass next to unmelted ice blocks, pistol shots frozen into a staccato Morse code, frost patterns on house exteriors which reveal the distribution of wall-furniture within, trees severed by machine gun bullets unexpectedly collapsing in a nightmarish landscape. Sjögren, in this novel, depicts an area of experience virtually untouched in the world of fiction, or at least seldom depicted so well.

Ultimately, as the title suggests, the novel is about love. The love of Plennik, the Russian prisoner, for Lúnnaja, the moon woman, has not only a dumb directness; Sjögren consecrates it with sacramental overtones and a bizarre lyricism. The Russian has what the two Swedish brothers do not have, as they recognize, namely the capacity for simple self-definition. National identity has nothing to do with it, of course, and Sjögren's anger over Arne Matsson's 1961 film version is understandable. The moving picture not only introduces alien elements, a scene where Stalin's portrait is shown hanging in a stable and another of Russians murdered by their own number hanging in clusters from the ice-laden trees; in addition Matsson apparently would have gone so far as to transform what Sjögren called "his beloved Russian" into a murderous villain, had not the author protested such distortion. Nonetheless the film was banned in Finland and incurred the wrath of the Russians at the Cannes Film Festival. In spite of all this, Sjögren grudgingly admitted that as a study of men under severe pressure it was impressive.

In *I Will Down to Thimnath* (*Jag vill gå ned till Thimnath*, 1947) Sjögren returns to a cluster of Swedes in a southern setting, this time Tunis, "white city of flies, confectioners, and consumption." The title comes from the Biblical fantasy of the late nineteenth-century Swedish poet Gustaf Fröding, "Spring" ("Vår"), in *Nya Dikter*:

> Lo, the lion of the desert
> seeks out his lionness;
> I will down to Thimnath
> and find myself a miss.

The "miss" at the heart of this concoction of politics and eroticism is Anna, a Småländsk *femme fatale*, with a potency of hysteria beneath her phlegmatic exterior. The men drawn into her orbit are: a druggist in flight into a world of opium and finally death in the Spanish Civil War; Beck, a Swedish-African photographer turned chicken farmer, who is married to an impressively physical French woman; the Becks' son Jean, who tries to conquer his inferior com-

xiv

plex in arms smuggling; and the central intelligence of the story, a Swedish legation officer. Ultimately the story is about the difficulty people have in establishing real human contact. As Stig Carlson puts it, "All the characters are night prowlers, who hide their deepest feelings from each other. A light veil of opium smoke wraps the whole story in a soft undulant envelope. Figures move about in insubstantial incarnations and moods and half-uttered opinions."

Sjögren launches the novel with an epigram from De Quincy: "Pure reason is the lowest trait in the human soul and that upon which man should least depend." The novel is not an explicit contrast between peripatetic Swedes and the Arab population, but the Arabs do come off very well. And yet Sjögren's intensity does not always save him from a kind of feckless romanticism. Of an earlier occasion, he wrote: "In Andalusia I met illiterates who stood on a higher cultural level than many manufacturers and good burghers of Småland." True enough, but there is a risk in idealizing them into a fictional community without much relevance to reality.

The next swing of the pendulum took Sjögren back to Sweden and the portrayal of a representative of the Swedish lower middle class, a tobacconist enlisted in a company of volunteers, where his motives are not so much dedication to the Finno-Russian War as those of escape from his own life of sick indecision and an impasse between two women, his wife Ruth, fat, garrulous, lonely, and ignored, and Cecilia (Cissi), wayward but fettered to her father. On a train moving northward toward the Finnish border, the tobacconist meets Cissi unexpectedly and she, in a moment of newly discovered freedom, commits herself to him. He jumps train in order to realize himself in this new life with Cissi, but drowns in a hidden pocket of icy water.

What is highly original about this novel, *The Man Who*

Tried to Bolt (*Mannen som försökte smita*, 1949), is the point of view, the angle of vision. Third-person narrative and first-person narrative are common enough, but here the mode of address is second person. The narrator sits at one end of a train car, only rarely — at the novel's beginning and end — calling attention to himself as "I." He continually addresses the protagonist at the other end of the car, in the manner of interior dramatic monologue as it were, with a mixture of distaste ("you sensed my antipathetic feeling for you") and sympathy. He does, in fact, intervene to the extent of trying to anticipate the disaster at the end. However, he is really outside the narrative. He does not know the tobacconist and yet he manages to reconstruct his whole life in these few hours on the train. He is the omniscient author practicing a kind of intrusive intimacy with no more justification than that of engaging our — the readers' — participation in the tensions of the story. The recurrent "you" has that effect. Nevertheless it is to the credit of Sjögren's indefatigable ingenuity that he attempts a bold and relatively uncommon point of view.[*]

One recent French novel, Michel Butor's *A Change of Heart* (*La Modification*, 1957) is interestingly similar. Butor's protagonist, also a peculiarly indecisive commercial agent, is on a 24-hour train journey. He is trying to decide between his wife, sagging with age and respectability, and his mistress, whose silken glow is easily equated with the free spirit of the future. Sjögren's "other woman" is Cecilia, Butor's is Cécile. Furthermore, in Butor the "you" mode is sustained throughout:

> You have chosen this compartment because the corner seat facing the engine and next to the corridor is vacant, the very seat you would have got

[*]See Bruce Morrissette, "Narrative 'You' in Contemporary Literature," *Comparative Literature Studies*, II (1965), 1–24.

Marnal to reserve for you if there had still been time, not the seat you would have asked for yourself over the telephone, since nobody at Scabelli's must know that it's to Rome you are escaping for these few days.

Finally, the focus in both novels is on attempted resolution and flight. I have no idea whether Sjögren influenced Butor (it seems unlikely), and I do not particularly care. In any case, Butor's success calls attention to Sjögren's failure. Butor's speaker never materializes as a separate identity. He is, in all probability, that aspect of the protagonist which attempts to view his real self by a distancing action (at the same time engaging the reader in the intimacy of the act by means of the somewhat extensible "you"). He is not necessarily split after the fashion of Prufrock ("let us go then, you and I); he is the disengaged, the rational self viewing the implicated, willess self. This is the struggle and the irony, and it plays no part in Sjögren. Nevertheless Sjögren's unremitting exploration of the narrative mode is one of his chief fascinations.

Lady (*Damen*, 1951), Sjögren's next novel, is as bleak and desolate in its world view as it is extravagant in its fantasy. The subjects are, again, the derelicts of the Spanish Civil War, and "the lady" of the title is, curiously enough, a chicken — a uniquely plumed chicken which represents fate, a kind of nervous destiny rounding the corner unexpectedly, pecking at the wounds of the deceased with that kind of grave, unstudied insouciance, or stupidity, so well exemplified in the poultry kind. Wounds. Wounds, physical and psychological, play a large part in Sjögren's gallery of grotesques. "The Pope," one of four characters, has had his upper lip split; and in performing an inept piece of home surgery — because he has no friends to come to his aid — he has created a series of blue-black swellings that make him look as if he were swallowing a rosary. Hence his nickname. But whatever the circumstances, Sjögren's characters have been wounded by life. They bear the stigma, or the stigmata, somewhere, without or within. *Det finns bara sårbarhet*, someone says in the novel. There is only "woundedness" or, rather, vulnerability.

The short stories in *The Confession* (*Bikten*, 1954) extend the uses of irony. "Flag at Half Mast" is a dramatic monologue somewhat after the pattern of Strindberg's "The Stronger," and it is, like so much of Sjögren's later fiction, as much a play as it is a short story. A woman locks herself in the home of her brother and forces him to listen to an account of how her husband hanged himself in front of one of those little Scandinavian table flags generally reserved for festive occasions. His fumbling with the flag in order to lower it to half-mast symbolizes his fumbling through all of life. Then, in a bloody denouement somewhat like that of Edward Albee's *Zoo Story*, she persuades (or forces?) the brother to bludgeon her to death with the blunt base of the flag pole. The "I" narrative, maintained throughout, creates a fascinating portrait of hysteria but obfuscates the ending, though perhaps according to design.

"Tears in Your Sleep," a short story in the same collection, is a good example of compact, anecdotal irony. A wagon tongue has been purloined to replace the pole of a tent occupied by a storm-battered unit during the Russo-Finnish War. The wagon driver enters the tent and inquires after the missing equipment while he is, at that very moment, leaning against it. Later, continuing his search, he freezes to death in the snow with his arms extended over his head and frozen into a rigid continuation of his body. The members of the unit sustain their grim practical joke by pre-empting the body for a tent pole (the cold presumably keeps it stiff) and the wagon tongue is returned to its rightful place. Survival demands all kinds of ingenuity, but the storyteller's ingenuity might very well be called into question, were it not supported by sharp circumstantial detail, edged dialogue, and an unforgettably dramatic visual image at the end.

Sjögren frequently taxes the limits of plausibility in just this fashion. Many of his fictive devices skirt the brink of the absurd and are defensible only because they are part of a total vision of life as incongruity. Or because they represent a probing curiosity to see whether life looks as absurd through other eyes.

In *Take Down the Stars* (*Ta ner stjärnorna*, 1957), an intrigue story about a criminal act at sea — the scuttling of a ship for the insurance money — the action is conveyed in its entirety through the first-person account of a woman who has to do some eavesdropping more implausible than anything to be found in Restoration comedy, in order to keep the reader properly informed. Would not Sjögren have been well advised to stick to the greater mobility of the omniscient author? Granted that Sjögren wants to portray a wholly authentic person in a world of artifice. But the authentic person is, in fact, the deceased mother of Hillevi, the narrator, who is a lively presence in the memories of all the principals. Hillevi is a part of the artifice; life teaches her little and she confesses her emptiness at the end of the novel as she drifts on to new sexual encounters. On the other hand, her promiscuity gives her a measure of insight:

> So bottomlessly childish, so indolent (not only in
> the movements of his body), and so stubbornly
> credulous is man!

And her response to the total masculinity about her, indeed the sensual presence of either sex, heightens perception (the shape of hands and the sound of heels) and magnifies this life of artifice. Her knowing compliance with aimless sensuality validates the manner of telling. Is anyone left who has some hope for the future, who is not trapped in the eternally recurring physical present, with only vague, alcoholic nostalgias for the vital past? Is there anyone who can still "take down the stars"?

In spite of his evocative descriptive powers, Sjögren has been increasingly insistent that his characters tell their own story. In *Memory* (*Till minne*, 1959) consists of four dialogues, essentially unrelated but loosely assigned to the four stages of man. "In Memory of the Child," or "The Glass Factory" as it was called in radio production (9 August 1961), is a fantastic conversation between a half-grown, precocious boy and his great-grandfather who was reportedly kicked to death by a horse. "In Memory of the Youth," "Young in Paris" in its Swedish radio version (4 October 1960), depicts an encounter between a hungry, callow, inept Swedish intellectual, with a hero-worship of Henri Rousseau, and a Parisian *midinette*. The dialogue burns with a surreal flame comically punctuated by the girl's rebuffs ("Stop that. Take your hand away."). With a presiding irony typical of Sjögren, "In Memory of the Man" depicts the conversation of two starving military couriers on their way to deliver a food package in some arctic no man's land. "In Memory of the Old Man," bizarrest of them all, is a conversation between an aging dancer and the gravedigger who is burying the ashes of his late wife and partner. Presumably it is both the withholding action of the play and the intensification of irony that have made Sjögren turn increasingly to drama as his favored medium, because he is clearly not much interested in the possibilities of stage spectacle which have appealed to Swedish playwrights from Strindberg to Werner Aspenström. It is for this reason that his plays have lent themselves particularly well to the radio. Or is it that, because the radio play is still a living literary form in Sweden, he has been increasingly drawn to its aesthetic demands?

The case of Sjögren in Sweden is not unlike that of Harold Pinter in England. Both are aware of the public insistence on verification, an insistence that realistic drama often supplied in easy ways. Life is only grudgingly verifiable. There are always the dark expanses of mystery, the large areas of silence, that lie just outside communication and, often enough, are interspersed within it. The purely auditory experience of radio accentuates this human condition. The strategy of word deployment on the printed page, which Sjögren uses in his later story-plays, can merely suggest what is a vital reality in spoken form.

In *Elis* (1964), Sjögren demonstrates that the typographical idiosyncrasies of his later books are far from whimsical or rhetorical, but part of a total poetic conception. *Elis* is, in fact, a novel in free verse, occasionally verging on hexameters, where the narrative is stylized without loss of rustic humor or colloquial bite. It is a genre picture of life around a Småland glass factory in the twenties, but it is more. Knut Ahnlund goes so far as to call it "an epic, a myth of man's degradation and his fellowship in misery."

Elis is partitioned into two halves depicting the life and death of the title character. The first half says much less about the three-year-old Elis than it does about the sterile couple, Frans and Iris, who have provided him a home and patched a life together out of a diseased, abject beginning to their marriage. The second half focuses upon the eighteen-year-old Elis, returned from a life of dope-pushing in the Chicago area, to a confrontation with his real mother and a suicide which compounds accusation, expiation, and the appropriate realization of the absurd.

As usual with Sjögren, there is an involution of narrative process (in contrast to the simple chain-reaction of tale-telling in Isak Dinesen). This time the narrator is an orphaned Finn, Toiwo Nikkala, who grows up in Småland, where he hears and overhears the first part of the story, and then comes to a bad end in America, under death sentence in some Wisconsin jail, at the end of the second part. Aside from Sjögren's fairly rudimentary conception of the United States, one wonders about the wisdom of conveying all information so circuitously — and through a dubious intelligence at that. In a letter of 1 December 1964, Sjögren reassures us that for material reasons he was forced to publish the novel prematurely and that the second section, only sketched in, remains to be converted into full canvas. The resultant diptych, with character deepened and point of view clarified, should add substantially to Sjögren's stature as an artist.

Even in Scandinavia Sjögren's reputation is not yet established. Some critics dismiss him as an artful technician; others, and some of the most perceptive, argue that he is a great stylist who should command more respect than he does. The crux may very well be a duality of mind and motivation. Perhaps the problem is that Sjögren's originality lies in an attempted merger of two apparently antagonistic forms, the detective story and the dream fantasy, or at least a kind of grotesquerie not far from the surreal. Logic is essential to one, illogic to the other. Incremental revelation to one, hallucination to the other. A kind of meeting ground is established in *Bread of Love* and for that reason it remains the most satisfying of Sjögren's novels.

RICHARD B. VOWLES

8 July 1965

xxii

BIBLIOGRAPHY

BY PEDER SJÖGREN

Bar Barbar. Stockholm: Bonniers, 1937. (Reportage.)
Svarta palmkronor (Black Palms). Stockholm: Medéns,
1944; Vingförlaget, 1952; Folket i bild, 1958. (Novel.)
Kärlekens bröd (Bread of Love). Stockholm: Medéns,
1945; Folket i bild, 1954. (Novel.)
Jag vill gå ned till Thimnath (I Will Down to Thimnath).
Stockholm: Medéns, 1947; Tidens bokklub, 1956.
(Novel.)
Mannen som försökte smita (The Man Who Tried to Bolt).
Stockholm: Norstedts, 1949. (Novel.)
Damen (The Lady). Stockholm: Norstedts, 1951. (Novel.)
Bikten (The Confession). Stockholm: Norstedts, 1954.
(Short stories.)
Ta ner stjärnorna (Take Down the Stars). Stockholm:
Norstedts, 1957. (Novel.)
Till minne (In Memory). Stockholm: Norstedts, 1959.
(Four dialogues.)
"Vårt nummer" ("Our Number"). *Svenska radiopjäser.*
Stockholm: Sveriges radio, 1959. Pp. 135–45. (Radio
play.)
"Högmodet" ("Pride"). *Dödssynderna: Sju enaktare (The
Deadly Sins: Seven One-Acters).* By Per Edström *et al.*
Stockholm: Bonniers, 1959. Pp. 57–68. (Radio play.)
"Möte i parken" (Meeting in the Park"). *Svenska radio-
pjäser.* Stockholm: Sveriges radio, 1962. Pp. 203–19. (Ra-
dio play.)
Elis. Stockholm: Norstedts, 1964. (Novel.)

Ahnlund, Knut. "Peder Sjögren." *Svenska dagbladet*, 30 November 1964.

Björkman-Goldschmidt, Elsa. "*Bikten*." *Vänkritik: 22 samtal tillägnade Olle Holmberg*. Stockholm, 1959. Pp. 225–31. (Essays on divers authors by divers hands.)

Meurling, Per. "Kärlek och död hos Peder Sjögren." *Ord och bild*, 71 (1962), 220–25.

Nilsson, Olle W. "Peder Sjögren har fått nog av resor och Selma Lagerlöf." *Arbetaren*, 37 (1958), 4. (Interview.)

Nordberg, Carl-Eric. "Vem är Tarsius? En studie i Peder Sjögrens författarskap." *Perspektiv*, 6 (1955), 362–67. Reprinted as "Peder Sjögren" in *Åtta udda: Prosa-profiler*. Stockholm, 1955. Pp. 113-34.

Runnquist, Åke. *Moderna svenska författare*. Stockholm: Forum, 1959. Pp. 99–100.

Veveris-Pehrsson, Dzidra. "Peder Sjögren och passivitetens problem." *Ord och bild*, 71 (1962), 225–31.

Wennberg, Gösta. "Ett motiv hos Peder Sjögren." *Bonniers litterära magasin*, 32 (February 1963), 140–43.

Bread of Love

CHAPTER 1

SIGNAL
AT DUSK

Everywhere it is like this now, men opening doors to report to women how a certain man died. In this case, he who died was the woman's son. He who enters is the comrade of the dead, who saw how it happened.

Women want to know all the details about how it happened. They sit tense as if reality were the greatest of all liars. They want to see the lie from every vantage point, as if they were only waiting to strike it down with a lightning blow and cry:

"It doesn't agree. There's a contradiction there. Then it isn't my son you're talking about. It's somebody else's. Mine's still alive — somewhere!"

They have known for months that he was dead, but they won't believe it.

I too walk into just such a woman's room, to do my duty and explain "how it happened." Not how just one man died, but two — two brothers.

I don't need to say who I am. I'm expected. We seat ourselves on either side of the table, an antique, lovely, treasured, rickety table. Nothing is on it but a slender little vase with a twig of mimosa. The mimosa is several days old. It has lost its freshness and the small berries are dry. They smell like straw. The mother is a small woman, in a silk blouse, thin and hollow-eyed. As she sits at the antique table, with her arms on the top and her thin chest lightly pressed on the table's edge, I notice a detail that shocks me into silence: the little woman's heart, also pressed against the table's edge, is beating so violently that its beat is conveyed to the table, and the flowers in the vase nod with each beat. The small mimosa berries rustle slightly and the sweet odor of straw is disturbed out of them.

I want to lie to her. It was I and nobody else who saw "how it happened." So I could lie any kind of story together — something impressive to make the old woman happy. But suddenly I realize that the black eyes directed at me would see through the least deviation from the truth. The black eyes directed at me like two pistol barrels. For a moment I'm irritated and say that I'm in a hurry and that in any case I can only say "how it happened" with one of the brothers, Tom, or Uncle Tom as we called him because he looked so much like a Negro. The younger, whom we never called anything but "the Bouncer," died alone, without witnesses. But in Tom's case, I know.

I begin to talk about the daylight out there, the daylight that never quite became light. We lived as if half blind, without light. Only for a couple of hours around midday, it was as if a giant spider, with some of its legs paralyzed, crept slowly toward the line of the horizon and ejected its viscous, rubber-colored web in the form of light, a sort of dull hangover light the color of wood lice. It never got very far, the spider of the horizon, it faltered more and more, and finally we were alone with the darkness, the cold, and the empty north woods all the rest of the day.

At just such a time, when the spider crept toward the horizon, we moved through the woods, I and my friend Tom. So I tell the old woman. We reached a place where the snow was white.

The old mother's eyes look reproachfully at me and I explain:

No, in the woods the snow wasn't always white. The fall of grenades had darkened it, so that it was almost entirely

4

black. But in one place the snow was white. It looked as if women were in the neighborhood and had spread sheets on the ground to dry. We could even smell the sheets, we always thought, just ironed, still damp and heavy, with the heavenly shimmer of the monogram sewn in silk by the pure hands of women. Tom had stopped for a moment and pulled out a small piece of paper with his mother's address on it. He extended it to me without saying anything. Immediately after, he crumpled and his great, heavy body fell in a heap, in the snow. There had been two sharp signals, just like the sounds announcing a long-distance telephone call.

But the mother doesn't understand. She says nothing. No sound comes from her throat, but her lips move precisely as if she were saying the words: "long-distance telephone call?"

Yes, that's the way it sounds in the woods. You have a weapon, I explain to her, a pistol that is much shorter than an ordinary rifle and shoots automatically, with unbelievable rapidity. The mechanism has the febrile sound of a telephone signal. Just as fast as the little hammer in the telephone apparatus beats against the two half-spheres, just that fast the pistol mechanism delivers its fire. So the fire is a signal.

Now the old woman begins to understand me.

Somebody was shooting at us, I continue. We didn't see him. My friend Tom was hit, not I. He wasn't hit by the first "signal," but by the second.

I sense that she wants everything in more detail, but there aren't many details. I don't quite know myself just why I thought it was the second "signal" that hit him, but I did.

When he was hit, I continue, he fell in a lying position.

I did too, of course; that's how it is when you're being shot at. We saw nothing, but we heard the man who fired on us escaping through the woods. He was on skis and the poles made a wild screeching in the snow, like swallows on a summer night.

He didn't die immediately, Tom, certainly not. But he didn't suffer either. I could tell by the way he talked. For he talked a great deal before he died.

The mimosa in the small vase quivers with each beat of her heart. It is as if I were holding in my hand an immature fledgling whose skin has not been completely covered with feathers yet. When you pick it up you can feel the pulsation of the little bird-heart against the inside of your hand.

Yes, he talked a good deal. But distracted, a little distracted as men do when they've been hit. Still, I understood him. Out there, men talk of the same things so often that you understand every hint of meaning. Anyhow, he talked about that signal that came toward us from the woods. He moved about in the snow a little as he talked, and I could see from his movements that he was badly wounded. But I couldn't help him. I could see that too.

Yes, he talked a good deal. About the signals. He wanted to say that they sounded just like the signals of a telephone, but that they hadn't frightened him the way telephone signals did.

The old woman strains herself to the utmost to understand me. Her whole body listens. Her face works, in small, small twitches, a different one for each of my remarks.

He tried to tell me, I continue, that he used to be surprised by angry signals when he was at home in his apartment. At dusk. Home in his attractive room. They struck him like whiplashes. He would crumple in a heap at the sound of those signals — malevolent, unexpected screams in the silence.

The signal that came from the automatic pistol scared him less. That was what he wanted to say. He didn't know that he was mortally wounded. They generally don't know. No, that scared him less. It wasn't heavy with dirt. It was purer. But the signals that struck him in the dusk at home in his apartment, from the insides of a telephone, could cripple him with evil apprehensions and awaken the smell of villains who would drop poison into his ears.

By now I have raised my voice and am uneasy and a little out of control. I ask if she understands me, but she remains silent and only shakes her fine head with a little smile of embarrassment. Then I tell it all over again and look at her as I finish. She has placed her gnarled, old mother-hands on the tabletop and tries to stand up, while her coal-black eyes observe me with hate as if in sharp denial that her son had enemies who wanted to get at him, as if to say that he was a noble man and a well-balanced man who hadn't the least kind of traffic with thugs.

Then I strike my forehead with impatience, and begin to pace back and forth in the room. I am quite aware that my voice is much too high for an ordinary room.

Good God, I shout, for the last time: men are crippled by loathsome suspicions when an unexpected telephone signal cuts through the darkness and the silence surrounding them. But when such a signal from an automatic pistol strikes you in such a darkness, you are not wounded in the heart! If you can't understand that, then I won't . . .

I am silent. My glance fastens upon the mimosa on the table. It is an almost comical sight — how it nods and shakes restlessly from the beat of her heart and sends out its odor of straw. Then I walk to her, take her hand, and kiss it.

Forgive me, I say. I lost control. But I want you to be-

7

lieve what I say. He died just as I told you. He crawled about in the white snow while he tried to say what I just said. There was no blood. Then, just as he stopped moving, he said: — Go to my mother.

I stand up without looking in her eyes. The last part, about carrying word to his mother, is a lie.

So I want to escape from the room in haste. I get as far as the door. And there I stop, quite immobile, with my back to the room and the old lady. It is an evening in spring.

Silent, everything is so silent. I shut my eyes. And I can still see the small mimosa berries quivering before me. And with that, all her aborted life inundates me, just as Tom once put it to me: the woman who never loved. Who expected that love would "come with the years." Who chose for herself a well-to-do man — a spiritual pedant — and then despised him in silence. And became despised in return. A man who tormented her endlessly, even from afar when he was not at home. A pedant of the type who does not hear the harmony in music, the spiritual tonality, but only the mechanical sounds coming from the instrument — metal disturbing metal, soft hammer against a steel wire, air passing through a half-opened brass aperture, stretched horsehair against gut. And in this way he perceived the symphony of existence. He didn't smell the redolence of anything nor see any beauty. — All her poverty forces itself upon me. I turn to the old woman and say:

But you must not believe that he died in vain. Through his death, all of us, his comrades, were saved. You must see that. He liberated all of us together. That is what he did.

She looks at me a long time. All that spring night we remain sitting at that antique, rickety table while I try to find some meaning in what I say.

8

CHAPTER 2

THE TABLE
WHICH IS
A BATTLEFIELD

During those silent, frightened seconds before I begin to tell my story to the old one, my deepest wish seems to be to arrange all the words so as best to strengthen and console her. But I don't do it because I can't. For any ordinary table, even if antique and valuable, separating two people sitting opposite each other on a spring night, can turn itself monstrously into a battlefield in the pallid night light.

It isn't necessary that one of the faces wishes to kill the other. But it may quite possibly be that one wishes to be killed, or at least wounded — and come very close to death. It can happen that one face provokes another to brutal, destructive thoughts and words without anyone's understanding how it can happen. Something indescribable in her impassive silence, a quick, dark shadow in her eyes, a hard, marble-white light over the bridge of her nose, or the unexpected scraping of her shoe soles on the floor — something irresistibly forces the destructive element into the face she is looking at. Because she is expecting it.

It can even happen that there are those who do not wish to wound, but only to be wounded. It may also be true that no one in his life — at the game's end — is senselessly mistreated. No one — except children.

And a tired, old woman may search out catastrophe — death in miniature — when her life seems warped, in order to put it straight again. The catastrophe seems to have at its service invisible tailors who know how to sew strait jackets on.

She can sit completely still, small, and transparent and force upon herself the certitudes of the suspicions a mother always defends herself against: That a mother never knows her own sons. That a mother knows nothing about them. That what she does know about them is false. That she sees in her sons only that which she condemned them to once long ago when they were children — or the result of that sentence. And instead the sons are everything they would have been had they never met their mother.

She can sit quite still, small and fragile, and with inconceivable strength force herself to the certainty that she gave life to two sons, but not the ability to live. And so they died for her.

CHAPTER 3

A WOMAN
SINGS
BY FULL MOON

I tell her that there was something "out there" that we loved because it was whole and complete and made us forget the viscous liquid light from the horizon-spider's spinnerets sticking to everything — the skin, the trees, the snow, and everything we ate. It was the moon. One night, shortly before Tom's death, the full moon was so intense that it blinded me. I stood quite still in the woods and even took a certain pleasure in being blinded. I wanted to laugh.

But, suddenly, the roots of my hair burned, as if from the goads of poisonous insects, with a powerful, childlike fear, and for some moments I didn't know where I was or what frightened me. First there was a dry, tittering sound, followed immediately by a soft rasping like the sail of a boat scraping the treetops, and then a crash, but muted, like a cosmic sigh, whereupon the moon disappeared. I had flattened myself immediately, and when the cold, almost air-light snow struck my face and was sucked into my nostrils like cocaine and made my forehead cocaine-clear, then I understood what had happened: one of the tall trees in the arctic woods around me had suddenly fallen, as if upset. It happened apparently without cause — or perhaps a slight, almost imperceptible night wind had felled the giant tree. The trees in those woods were all riddled with machine gun bullets and some were nearly sawed off just above the ground. They stood there defying the laws of nature, and it almost seemed that the draft from a flying owl could level great stretches of this silent, wilderness world.

I lay completely still while the fine snow that shot up at the tree's fall in dense, quick columns, darkening the moon, slowly settled. I had become so cautious about everything. And I wasn't the only one. Beside me lay my loyal companion, Tom, as still and immobile as I. But deep down inside I was suddenly slaphappy as one always is after a shock, although I imagined I was laughing at Tom. That unlucky fellow apparently had no idea what had happened, and so he had "cockroaches" in his throat — a kind of violent cough brought on by arctic air just at the time when absolute silence is called for. Poor, sweet Uncle Tom! That refined, reticent soul! For whom everything went wrong! Who was a revivalist preacher for half his life and incited mankind to a belief in God, until the moment when he discovered that he had no belief of his own. Until he found out that God is none other than life itself, daily living. And

11

belief isn't something you can just pick up. Either you get it from somewhere as a child, or you don't get it at all. Certainly, he had been a favored son, too much favored, and his forehead had been battered bloody out in the hardness of life. And it was his forehead that caught your attention when you looked at Tom — not the grey doglike eyes or the thick lips that made him look exactly like a Negro, although his greasy, sticky hair was ash pale. But his skin was dark out there in the woods where we lived in holes in the ground, probably because the icy clumps of earth that fell now and then from the shelter roof onto our heads, coloring them brownish-black, nine times out of ten fell on Uncle Tom, no matter where he sat. His bad luck seemed to be caused by something funny but equally frightening in his nature. His blackened forehead was pathetic — it looked hot, like a child's. The skin was uneven, in weals and protuberances, the fat lying in lumps underneath. And across that black and bumpy expanse shone the light red stripe made by his cap visor, like a scar from a whiplash.

Suddenly, lying there in the snow, I felt Tom's breath on my ear, and he whispered slowly:

"Do you see him?"

The question surprised me. Tom never talked unless he had to, and I'd noticed nothing around us. But the agitated clouds of snow had now subsided, leaving the view clear. Again everything was illuminated by the moon.

A little distance away, between us and the moon and in just that place in the snow formerly hidden by the fallen tree, was the silhouette of a large man. He stood quite still and cast a long, sharply defined moon-shadow. The shadow of his head extended as far as Tom and me, and I could have touched it with my hand. We lay just as still as before, because I saw clearly that it was as if his conical

12

headgear, with its peak, pointed right at Tom — the friendly little peak that meant he was Russian.

Whether his face was turned toward us or away from us it was impossible to decide. We just lay still, or almost still. The slight, chameleon-like motions of reaching for my automatic pistol would not have caught his attention even if he had been looking at me. The little clicking sound that a gun makes when you take it off safety couldn't have frightened him either. When it's below zero, the branches everywhere make metallic sounds as if they have a kind of audible gout. I could calmly, and with all the care which aiming in the moonlight demands, ambush the peak-headed one. But then I had to do it all over again. The spider webs that had draped the fallen tree, whitewashed with frost and softly hanging like lianas still floating in the air, came circling down and now settled gently on my gunsight. By the time I had drawn a bead again, the peakhead had moved. He had sunk into the snow as if laid low by a soundless shot. But he assumed a comfortable position on his knees and suddenly began to talk. I could see that his face was turned toward the moon and his hands were outstretched.

As it happens, I understand Russian. I first came here as an interpreter, but then became an ordinary soldier with a rifle company. Since he spoke in a loud voice and an easily understandable dialect, I began to listen to him. I soon gathered that he was not talking to any comrades near him in the woods. He was entirely alone. However weird it may sound, he was talking to a woman whom he loved intimately. Once, a long time ago, they had decided that if ever they were separated they would meet in the light of the full moon. They would in their own way, and wherever they happened to be, look into the face of the full moon as long as it lasted, and talk to each other. Tell about things that had happened to them, cheer each other up, and be together in heart. This invention seemed to delight him, and his voice, deep as it was rich, gave a continuous impression of intense experience, like rapture.

I whispered to Tom, in the midst of translating it all for him, that the man was probably a poor bugger who had got separated from his unit and was staggering about the woods a little dazed. But Tom, who had completely forgotten his "cockroaches," observed the foreigner with a deep, infectious solemnity and scarcely listened to me. For the most part the Russian could be clearly heard and I could not refrain from listening. One time he said:

"Tomorrow I'll be in Kámenka! Tomorrow I'll be with you in Kámenka!"

Kámenka was, or had been, a Russian village only a short distance from where we were. Before we passed through it, it was burned by the inhabitants who then followed their troops eastward. No one remained. Neither aged, nor women, nor children. I knew that. I had myself walked about the ashes and been astonished at small details: the farmyard chickens that now sat charred, grey-black, with heads twisted, as if they were shaped in clay by a sculptor; the hardware store's bicycles melted into a single, indistinguishable mass; and, only three meters away, old blocks of ice still unmelted, under a thin layer of sawdust; dog skeletons that suddenly disintegrated to small chalk-like heaps of dust. No, in Kámenka there was no longer anything left but chimneys, coal-black against the snow. We had spent hours there, creeping up on a cellar where voices had been heard. It was the Bouncer, Tom's sharp-eared brother, who swore that he heard them and reviled us when we didn't believe him. And it was he who volunteered to enter the cellar which turned out to be empty except for a sack of potatoes. The potatoes had been frozen, but the fire melted them and made them give forth a whispering, sighing sound, like mysterious, melancholy voices. No, in Kámenka there was no life.

Suddenly the peak-head was gone. First I felt duped by this clever rascal and ashamed of my credulity, but just as I was about to stand up, Tom pointed at something in front of us. It was white smoke rising from the snow, carrying with it a spark from time to time. Obviously the peak-head had found a hole or made a depression in the snow-cover where he intended to spend the night by a fire. Then he stood up again, casting his long shadow toward Tom and me, and he gave a low laugh as he talked to this woman, in the manner of a child, how he had run, he so tall and heavy and the snow so deep. He had abandoned his company only when he learned how near he was to Kámenka. He wanted to be back with his beloved, see her, talk to her, embrace her, and explain everything. Time after time in his flight he had evaded crucial sentry positions that fired at him, and, thinking of this, he raised the corners of his overcoat and pointed smiling to the bullet holes in them. He had small talk about the village, and I gathered that he had been a worker in the sawmill at Kámenka and that he thought the village was still standing even though enemy troops controlled the region. He said that he had expected to be in Kámenka that night and that he would have been if . . . Then he broke off and became silent. A moment later he twisted about abruptly as if he had suddenly discovered Tom and me, and came half-running straight toward us. I raised my automatic pistol again, but Tom remained motionless and only watched. The peak-head struggled out of his overcoat as he made his way with difficulty through the deep snow. I felt the powerful throb of my neck artery and a quick astonishment that no shot sounded in spite of the pressure of my finger on the trig-

15

ger. The joints had stiffened as they sometimes do after a period of inactivity in an arctic climate — as if the joint fluid had become as thick and glutinous as cheese.

The peak-head had stopped close to us. We heard his heavy gasps and clearly smelled the smoky odor of his clothes. He abruptly spread his coat over something in the snow and carefully covered it up. Then he returned to his hole.

I asked Tom, who lay nearer the coat, what the Russian could have been hiding, and Tom answered that it was somebody either killed or frozen, a man who had been clad in a full-length dogskin coat that the Bouncer had torn off him. One of the innumerable who had been left behind in the wood and whom we'd become accustomed to. They lay in grotesque postures, these dead, nearly all handsome young men with dry, black hair. Their leathery skin was a dark grey-brown, their heads and hands like sculptured sandstone. They were works of art. Just great works of art, eternal and unchangeable, though once they were men. The cold had hardened their clothing into cast iron. Everything was as hard as iron except the hair, the woolly black hair that occasionally fluttered over their immobility in some gentle breeze, and waved if one passed by in haste.

But Tom and I mused in vain at just what prompted him to warm a corpse with his cloak, and in fact his whole behavior so fascinated us that we could not leave, in spite of the cold which intensified with every moment that passed.

Once again he disappeared in that astonishing way, and the air began to glow redly from his foxhole fire. For awhile he was invisible, but we could still hear his voice raised as if to drown out the crackling of the wood. He was telling the woman that everything had gone well for him. There was only one night when he had suffered from the cold a

16

little, he said. But then he had stumbled upon a reindeer cow. She lay in the snow, her back legs shining blackly with blood, for she had stepped on a mine. Her horns were very small. She lay with her cloven hooves spread wide, and, when she now and then pressed them against the snow as if she dreamt she was standing up, a snapping sound came from the hooves — and he imitated the sound, first with the tongue and then with the fingers. In the vicious cold of that night he had lain next to her, because there was no dry wood for burning. First he had stuck his hands in her whiskers. Then he had buried his face and arms in the long mane that covered the underside of her neck. He stuck his legs in the hairiness of her belly. So he lay. Sometimes she lifted her head and looked at him. Her eyes had white rings about them. Toward morning the reindeer died. She'd given him rest and prevented him from freezing to death. Then he cut flesh from her body and took it with him. He didn't need to starve. He grilled it over the fire.

As he finished talking, he clambered out of the hole. He was holding out a piece of meat that had clearly been cooked over the fire. He showed it to the woman and said that it tasted fine. Then he sat down in the snow and put the meat to his mouth. The fire, which had now flamed up, illuminated him so that, now, there was something about him that moved Tom and me deeply. His hands were still so cold that he fumbled helplessly with the meat. He didn't seem to understand fully why the meat did not reach his mouth, however much he tried. The breath from his nostrils had frozen into two icicles and hung from his unshaven upper lip like heavy walrus tusks over his mouth. When he realized what the problem was, he looked perplexed and explained that if you removed the tusks they would take pieces of face with them. He gave a low, embarrassed laugh and made the woman promise that she absolutely would

17

not worry about his welfare. Everything was all right, and the fire would soon enough melt the icicles away. He stuffed the meat into his pocket, took off his cap, and asked the woman to sing for him. He wanted her to sing the song of the *prosphorá*, the blessed bread, their own love song which he treasured more than anything else on earth. While she sang, he stood quite still with bared head and listened devoutly. He was clearly outlined against the rose-colored air over the fire hole, a nimbus which, like the imaginary song, rose and fell and took on animation. And when I thought of the black, cold emptiness that would meet him in Kámenka, I decided that he must die happy. But then Tom took a look at the skies and announced that it was going to be the coldest night yet. The fire would silently dwindle in the hole with the tired man. There would be no dawn for him. He would be lying in his hole precisely like thousands of others in that forest — hard as stone. Only a work of art.

Then we stood up and left the place. Our windbreakers had frozen as we lay there and they cracked with the same sound that a newly lit fire makes, but we walked away without troubling whether he heard us or not. The moon had traveled a bit and the forest was a new one, not at all like the old. With changing light conditions, we should never have been able to find our way, without the help of the dead. We had made up names for many of them, and in that way we could identify places in the woods and what direction to take. We felt some gratitude toward these "works of art," this expanse of calm and truth.

Tom and I passed slowly among them and from time to time glanced upward at the full moon, as if to discover whether the peak-head's beloved was still there. And, somehow, we knew she was. The burnished moon surface was so full of life, play, beauty, curiosity, and song.

We did not stop until we happened to see the gleam from a peculiar, sulfur-yellow ice formation that resembled a small stalactite grotto and was formed by the urine of soldiers on the bushes, frozen and suspended in mid-air. It was then we decided to say nothing at all about the peak-head. Our relief chief Ledin would punish us severely if he learned that we had let a Russian run free in our woods without "de-activating" him.

From the place of the phosphorescent grotto we could see four pillars of fire, as thick as a man's arm and a half meter high, rising straight up from scarcely perceptible swellings in the snow cover. The fire columns were perhaps thirty meters from each other and they came from small dugouts, *korsu*, where soldiers lay packed in tightly together. The fires meant that for the time being there was enough fuel for the small rectangular iron boxes that passed for stoves, and, most important of all, that no Russians were thought to be about, since these pillars of flame, rising from stubby sheet-metal mouths, were a dead giveaway. But we — the twenty-odd men occupying the woods — had very little idea how much care to exercise. We knew nothing. We were completely out of contact with our company. We didn't know what had happened and what was happening around us. And we couldn't leave that spot.

Tom and I lived with the Bouncer and Ledin, a sergeant and the leader of the group, under the fire column farthest to the right. We were all volunteers. All you had to do was open a small door of cardboard with spruce tacked to the outside, and jump in. The little hole, with its dark-red earth walls, was abandoned and empty when we arrived, but the fire in the iron box was so hot that two walls glowed redly and provided light enough so that the carbide lamp hanging from one of the beams was not needed. We silently struggled out of our windbreakers and ski boots, put them

outside so that the cold would freeze the sweat to ice —
they warmed up better then — and stretched out on the
floor to sleep. But for a long time we lay there with our eyes
wide open. Finally I asked:

"What are you thinking about, Tom?"

His answer was straightforward:

"Her."

It was the first time that the woman, whom I had, in my
fantasy, christened Lúnnaja, moon woman, entered our
poor little hole which the earth walls and the spruce on
the floor made smell exactly like a grave.

CHAPTER 4

THE TIRED
GUEST

Out there we had got in the habit of never sleeping for
very long at a time. And we slept for no more than about
an hour after that experience with the crashing tree. We
awoke simultaneously, Tom and I. At that moment I had
the feeling that someone silently sat and looked at me. And
so it was.

I hardly dared believe in the face I saw turned toward
me. I had never really seen it clearly before, but merely
sensed it; it was, nevertheless, all too well known to me:
it was Peak-Head. The Russian. He was inside our hole and
sat and looked at me.

The carbide lamp on the ceiling burned with a hissing
sound. Its blue-white light cast a pitch black shadow from
the stranger's nose, which was enormously large but well

shaped nonetheless, a nose that might have been borrowed from a circus giant. He was, in fact, no giant, even though he appeared so, clad in that wide-flaring coat we had seen him in against the moonlight. He looked powerful and tough, but not especially tall. I couldn't see his mouth and chin because they were obscured by the deep shadow cast by his nose, but I did see his eyes and they captured me immediately. They were very light. When you meet men like that, out in full daylight, it's as if their eyes were holes right through the head and what you see is a light, airy spring sky far behind the man. He stared at me, in an open, friendly fashion, but as if he was completely exhausted. He sat very close to the rectangular oven where there was still a fire. I could tell that the heat, which he must have been quite unaccustomed to, had got into his blood and dazed him. He looked as if he wouldn't hear anything if he were spoken to, in spite of the fact that his eyes were open. I don't know what made me suddenly start to ask him in Russian what the idea was of wrapping a dead man in his cloak, but just as I was about to say it, the Russian slowly began to fall to one side, to collapse, in precisely the same silent way that the tree had done out in the woods. It seemed as if he were deep asleep in the midst of his fall, even before his head reached the spruce on the floor and perhaps even before he shut his eyes. And he lay there.

But in just that place which had been hidden by all his bulk — just as it was with the tree — Tom and I saw another figure and one better known to us: the Bouncer. With his back against the earth wall, partly hunched into a little niche, he sat or half lay there, like an entirely new man, a figure with the aura of a stranger. He was so utterly changed since we saw him last that Tom exclaimed:

"God in heaven, is it you?"

But we needed no more than the exchange of a glance, Tom and I, to know what had happened.

The Bouncer had always seemed to us the prototype of those hunks of men installed at the entrances of bars, clumsily gross and yet with something of a doll's harmlessness about his whole person. Back in those days before Tom had joined us, the Bouncer had been silent, humble, a little dreamy, and almost shy. Everybody had somehow felt sorry for him and his colossal arms and legs at such a young age — well, hardly twenty-five anyway. You wanted to help him move them. But then he began to turn into an entirely different man: arrogant, a little condescending, threatening, better than the rest — in short, an egotist and a bully. It didn't suit us at all. Some among us were worse than the Bouncer, in one way or another, and we let them alone. But we gave the Bouncer hell. Even if he thought just as others thought, even the stupidest among us said that the Bouncer was wrong and the others were right. All he had to do to be attacked was simply to appear.

But the Bouncer took up the battle. Stubbornly — and perhaps heroicially — he fought for his inflated ego. He wouldn't part with it. He defended the unsympathetic side of himself. Oh, sometimes he wavered. When it was clear that his "well-meant" designs were a mistake or that he wasn't as strong as his limbs suggested — he was actually quite weak — then he folded up for a time, with a humble, deep sorrow in his eyes that were "brown as bedbugs and just as cheeky," and he responded without a word or a grimace to the abysmal contempt that we all showered upon him. But then he could sigh a short, peculiar sigh that sounded exactly like snow about to turn into water when it's in a cup on the stove. After that he'd recover quickly and begin to stride around, pleased with the disagreeable stench of his black fur coat, and he'd say:

"What got into you just now, fellas? Getting a little tense already? More guts needed, huh?"

His humility had stayed with him about a week last time, that is to say, since the day he swore the potatoes spoke Russian in that cellar in Kámenka. His nose had been rubbed in those potatoes so thoroughly that it almost hurt to look at him. For a whole week he avoided everyone, said nothing, and sighed frequently like snow beginning to melt.

Anyhow he now sat in the niche with a dogskin coat over his shoulders and exuded self-assurance. His eyes were directed steadily and with some sympathy first at Tom, then at me, and then at his own nose which had changed, had in fact grown and was twitching uneasily since it was frost-bitten and did not thrive in the neighborhood of the stove. He had to squint somewhat in order to see it, but the brown gaze lost nothing of its smugness: in front of him lay Peak-Head.

Into that already insufferably crowded hole the Bouncer had come, dragging with him a prisoner.

CHAPTER 5

THE BREAD
THAT SHOWED
THE WAY
TO A HEART

The Bouncer's expansive satisfaction at taking a prisoner became less disturbing as the nights passed. Our lair, with its tomblike smell, was painfully crowded and the Bouncer himself had to sit in his niche in the earth wall. When he was sure that everybody was asleep, he allowed himself to sigh laboriously and sometimes attacks of cramps twisted his great legs. But in the daytime he gave the appearance of being at peace with the world. He would move around imitating Ledin, and he always wore a gun on each shoulder — one double-barreled, in case he should come upon a rabbit or a bird — and looked particularly warlike. The thing that amused him most was the way the less hardy soldiers were suffocated by the smell that came from his black fur coat. He was still a long way from humility. Particularly as it soon became apparent that we got a good deal of use and pleasure out of the prisoner.

From the beginning the Russian maintained a quiet reserve and never mingled in anything that didn't concern him. He ate nothing unless he was told to and unless the food was placed in his hands. He asked no questions, not even about Kámenka — as far as that goes, our commander had forbidden us to talk to the prisoner about the village. During the hearing, the prisoner responded most cooperatively, in a friendly and straightforward fashion. But he didn't know much, not even how he had wandered into our hands. We were surrounded by a mine belt, and how he penetrated it was inexplicable to him as well as to us. A light snowfall the day after his arrival had obliterated his tracks completely. Otherwise it appeared that he had only one wish, to be useful. We set him to work watching the stove, cutting wood, and melting snow. He took care of everything like a faithful old watchdog. We soon came to trust him enough to use him as an aircraft lookout. His ear was sharp and so was his vision. It was touching how anxious he was to warn us of enemy planes in good time. Recently it was only planes that disturbed our isolation. He was as dependable as a listening machine and seemed to

24

know instinctively when something was going to happen. He would lumber around from hole to hole gesticulating with his great, black hands, full of a kind of thoughtful intensity. When he was rewarded with a half-smoked cigarette, he would bow with painful politeness. He was also a very capable cook. One day he went out in search of that reindeer corpse that I had heard him telling the moon about, and cut out a quantity of frozen meat which he dragged home to us on a *pulka* that he had fashioned out of spruce branches. During the meal he kept asking us: Well, how does it taste? Or: What can you expect, under the circumstances? Or: I don't suppose you want me to fetch any more for you, do you? And after every question, he peered at us with a kind of guarded curiosity through his little eyes that shone like a light spring sky and looked from one to the other of us — Tom, the Bouncer, and me.

How we ate and drank that evening! We had wood, carbide, meat, and vodka. The vodka Tom had collected from the pocket flasks of the dead Russians scattered thickly about the woods. The prisoner became talkative from the liquor and asked us to call him Plennik, which quite simply means "prisoner." I interpreted and asked him to give a full account of the dead man who had owned the dogskin coat and for whom he sacrificed his cloak in the woods. He laid the cloak over him, he confessed with some embarrassment, so that his woman wouldn't be disturbed by such a sight in the moonlight. She knew the dead man. He was from Kámenka too.

Plennik — the prisoner, that is — said that he had been away from Kámenka for all of twenty years, in fact since the first war. When he returned several years ago, he was forty years old. He returned one cold, windy autumn evening, he said, and he was starved and frozen through. The village was entirely changed. None of his old friends were left, no relatives, no one who knew him. People had changed character, he said, and they all looked at him with suspicion. They were afraid of him and hastened to lock their doors in his face. That evening he gave up all hope and all faith in life. But then life came back to him. He died, he said, and was reborn.

He described Kámenka for us. The village lay in the middle of an open swampland where no tree grew, not even a bush. The woods were thick and warm around the swamp, but in the flat village itself it was always colder than anywhere else. Precisely in the center of the swamp, where the rivers Bjélaja and Chalódnaja converged, lay Kámenka with its dark, low log cottages and smokehouses. The autumn day he arrived it was so cold that all the inhabitants had moved into their kitchens to keep warm. You can see such a thing from the outside, because parts of the wall are chalkwhite against the usual black of the unpainted outer surfaces. The warmth from the heated room penetrates the walls and causes a layer of luminous white rime frost on the outside. On such a day you could see from a distance, in fact from the edge of the woods, where the wall-fast furniture was located. He had walked around looking at the houses and then wandered down in the direction of the river, on the point of tears. But then he suddenly stopped and pricked up his ears like an animal. His nostrils had detected a smell that reminded him of something. It was the odor of dog — the strong, rank smell of dog. Just that moment something dark and about his size had moved past him. It was a man dressed in a dogskin coat which was quite black and reached almost to his feet. He moved soundlessly because he wore *ónutji*, or white rags, wrapped around his legs and feet. Earlier that evening a man in just such a coat had given him a blank stare when Plennik had asked for something to eat, and now he felt a sudden hatred for the stranger and his dog smell. A hatred stronger than any he had felt before. A hate that he was aware of but could not control. And he suddenly noticed that he had a heavy weapon in his hand, a stone. He really had no idea whether he wanted to rob the stranger, take revenge upon him, or merely take from him that long, stinking coat. But in that instant one thing became clear to him: it was his own life he wanted to destroy, and not someone else's.

He stood by an old oven which had been used for smoking fish, and waited for the man with the dog smell. Nobody else was about. It was dark, except for a small lantern which threw a weak, yellow light for a few meters around it. When the man in the fur coat took quite a different direction from that which Plennik had anticipated, he had to take a shortcut. But he miscalculated. The man wandered about irrationally, almost as if he were trying to fool someone. It irritated Plennik. He no longer had the patience to keep hidden behind the woodpile where he was now standing, but wanted to rush forward and do the job without any precautions whatsoever. But just at that moment the man turned and came straight toward Plennik without seeing him. They were quite close to the river, near a small wooden quay. The edge of the quay was only a step from where Plennik stood, and the dogskin man would have to go close, very close to him. He approached, and came into the pale circle of light from the quay lantern, walking slowly with his head thrust forward into the gusty evening wind. The river was not entirely frozen over since it was still autumn, and the convergence of the two streams caused currents and whirlpools. Two or three lights shone weakly from a houseboat on the other side of the river and from that same point came the voice of a man singing.

The dogskin man approached slowly. Plennik stood with the rock raised over his head. The wind blew and the lantern light seemed to shrink as if it didn't want to watch. Only one step more. One step. Then the man stopped. Right in front of Plennik.

He did not stop as if he had discovered Plennik or sensed danger. He stopped quite calmly, as if during his whole erratic walk his intention had been to stop at just that point. The dog smell stabbed at Plennik's nostrils and his only thought was that it was exactly the same smell he had noticed earlier when he had been turned away. The man stood stock-still looking at something in the river that completely captured his attention.

Plennik himself looked out over the river and discovered an object. The ice extended only a few meters from the quay edge, and then open, black water took over. The object, which was no bigger than an open hand, lay on the ice. Plennik couldn't tell at first what it was, but when the lantern light flamed up for a moment, he decided it must be a piece of bread, a little round bread of a special kind — a *prosphorá*, holy bread blessed by a priest. Some kindly soul had put it out on the ice for the birds.

The man in the dogskin coat stood for a long time looking at the bread, as if he couldn't turn away. Suddenly he glanced about to see that no one was watching. He was completely unaware of Plennik and his raised arm.

The man moved. Not toward Plennik, but toward the bread. He went down to the quay edge, squatted by the piles, looked around once more to see that nobody was watching, and then began to let himself down awkwardly and laboriously to the ice.

Plennik slowly lowered the stone. He now understood that the other man suffered from hunger too. His anger disappeared and he only stood and watched.

After he had got a foothold, the man carefully tried the

ice's strength. Once, when the ice gave a dull, unexpected sound, Plennik jumped and made a noise. Both men were frightened. The man on the ice reassured himself once more that no one was about. Then he continued toward the bread. The ice was weak, but the bread drew him on.

Plennik was no longer so immobile. He had discarded the stone and his hands opened and shut as if they were eating the air, and he breathed in gasps, all the while ready to jump out on the ice — not to hurt the man but to help him.

It wasn't necessary. The man reached the bread, stretched out his hand, and got hold of it. But it was frozen fast!

It was completely imbedded in the ice! And then, oh merciful God, the man on the ice was seized by irrational violence like that Plennik had just known. He began mumbling to himself and kicking at the ice in order to release the bread. Then the ice broke.

It happened suddenly. He sank gently and without a sound. He disappeared completely, but only for a moment, Then he shot up as if propelled from below. An almost circular piece of ice had separated from the mass, with the bread at the center, like a handle. Even then the man couldn't forget that wretched piece of bread. He stretched out his arm and got hold of it once more. The ice fragment was strong enough at least to hold him up.

But the current had caught it and carried it out into the stream. Plennik sprang from his hiding place. It was as if someone threw him into the river, precisely where the fragment had been. He went deep under, deeper than the other, and came to the surface. He fought with all his strength against the fluid cold about him and moved out toward the block of ice.

The current was strong and full of whirlpools caused by the convergence of the two streams. But he reached the spinning fragment, and in spite of the weight of the cold water he was able to reach his arm up and get hold of the bread. But the other screamed at him:

"Let go of the bread! It's mine! I saw it first! It's holy bread — and a sin to throw it out on the ice!"

He fought for the bread as if it were a precious stone. He exhausted himself completely and understood none of Plennik's efforts to calm him. Then, suddenly, he became less agitated and said:

"I don't want it for myself. The bread. But for the wife of our *nadsmótrtjik*, our overseer. It's holy bread and nothing for birds!"

Then he was silent. The ice had floated a long way from the quay lantern and Plennik could see nothing at all. After a time it penetrated his frozen brain that the other had let go. Plennik called out, louder and louder, but got no answer.

The singing from the barge had stopped. His voice had been heard, and a couple of men came out and called back. They jumped into separate skiffs and rowed quickly out toward Plennik. One of them, an old man with a bushy red beard, picked up Plennik and took him to the barge where he was offered brandy and a bunk for the night. The other bargeman, who was younger and stronger, stayed out in the river looking for the man in the fur coat. And he found him. The coat had held up its owner after cold and exertion had robbed him of all strength. The bargeman helped him home.

But Plennik had stubbornly hauled the ice fragment to the barge and there cut the bread out with an axe. He had got it into his head that he must deliver it to the wife of the overseer. The next day he would make every effort to locate her.

And he did. And as he told his story — our dear prisoner,

30

there in our den — he smiled with a good deal of embarrassment, and looked from one to another of us as if to ask pardon for having tired us. Then he went on to explain: "Anyway, now you know how I came to meet the man who's lying out there with my cloak over him. But not only that. Now you know how I found my woman, my dear, beautiful wife in Kámenka. It was to her that the bread led me. It was she who was the overseer's wife. She whom you have come to call Lúnnaja."

He stood up and as he began to open the frozen little cardboard door in the ceiling, he said solemnly:

"Lúnnaja is a good name for her. A fine name. I'll call her that myself. Because she's not earthbound. She believes in love, and people don't very often. But she believes blindly. Maybe you can understand. You know how I came to her. Poor, frozen, almost a beggar, almost a — murderer. I told her everything. But she loved me immediately, without asking about anything else."

And then Plennik smiled and clambered out, as eagerly as if she awaited him out there in the frozen forest.

CHAPTER 6

A FACE

IS SUDDENLY

CHANGED

Yes, this is what I tell the little mother at the table with the mimosa on it, the — circumstances of her sons' deaths, Tom's and the Bouncer's. It has become dark but we have not lit the lamp. The spring night is motionless outside the

31

windows. A trace of light remains on her face. But it suddenly seems that her face has changed, and the change frightens me a little. It happened just when I said that about Lúnnaja, that she "believed blindly" in love. I try to remember if I said it in any special way, in any special tone of voice. I don't know. But a brief pause has arisen in the story, and I hasten to continue. However, as I continue, I know what it was that I sensed during that interruption. I realize that it was precisely there that the old woman's unhappiness lay, that she had never believed in love.

It is so. Men have scarcely discovered love yet. Not that it's so especially significant. But nature does not seem to have the power to forgive a woman who chooses her husband for reasons other than love. Nature is grim that way.

It is the woman who gives the invitation to love. It is she who invites the man by not thrusting him away. Perhaps she is not herself conscious of ceasing to rebuff him. It happens in an infinitely more subtle way than with words, thoughts, and glances.

No woman has the power to leave the man she has so chosen — if he gives her all the love she expects of him. For once she has chosen, it is no longer she but he who is the power in their love. His love is a thick smoke that clothes her like a garment. She cannot remove it. She can never step fragilely naked out of it.

The old face changed precisely at that moment when I talked about "believing blindly" in love. Her face became so frighteningly like her son's — Tom's. I had thought that her lips were thin, but they suddenly appeared full. I could see then that she had loved Tom more than anything else in her life.

One never knows, but perhaps a man and a woman must love each other utterly, utterly, for the fruit of their love to live — not merely to be born but to live. No one can pretend to a child. The child is more sensitive than thought itself. And no one can force himself to love. No one can deceive love, however clever he may be.

CHAPTER 7

THE WOMAN
IN THE
RED GLOW

Through the mist, under a palely shimmering aurora borealis, an animal followed me. It was a remarkable little animal that for nearly half an hour kept at a distance of four or five meters and sometimes stretched itself to three times its length or divided itself in two, as it seemed, or took the form of a ball, now bouncing, now gliding softly, close to the surface of the snow. I was on my way to Kámenka on skis, alone, and had to take a path lined on both sides with the cadavers of horses. They lay with their legs stretched straight and stiff in the air, like bizarre signposts.

I could see the animal that followed me but could scarcely believe in its reality. After all, there aren't any animals that can elongate themselves that much or turn into balls rolling soundlessly over the snow. I banished the unpleasant impression of the animal's presence by concentrating on my purpose: I must get hold of Plennik — Plennik, who had seen fit to disappear. It happened the day after the reindeer feast. He had made off in the afternoon, nobody knew where or how. Ledin, our relief chief, was furious.

Ledin, a sergeant, lived with me, Tom, the Bouncer, and Plennik in the hole farthest to the right. Nobody really knew

33

what went on in his mind. He was a grey-eyed man of some thirty years who always kept himself well shaven and displayed that grimness of countenance which is so desirable in the professional soldier, a grimness further emphasized by short, barely discernible muttonchop whiskers. Although Ledin was apparently satisfied with his decorative military appearance — he had besides a scar on his forehead that looked like a saber wound but actually came from being kicked by a horse — and although he was sometimes overly infatuated with his compact, broad-shouldered figure, still he was a commander whose slightest nod we obeyed and with whom we all wanted to be on good terms. Plennik also had been anxious for Ledin's favor, but without success. What Ledin had against him, or suspected him of, nobody understood. But every time he looked at the Russian his face unconsciously twisted into something vulgar, cynical, or ugly, as if a bit of bitter almond had got stuck in his teeth. Plennik harbored an intuitive, meek fear of Ledin, and the two of them never looked each other in the eye.

Now Ledin was beside himself. On such occasions he had a way of walking that was both tense and exaggeratedly poised; otherwise you could detect nothing. His voice and eyes were friendly, quite as if he were grateful for the fury concealed within him. There could be no other cause now than Plennik's disappearance. Not much happened in our icebound woods. Everything was as paralyzed as the nauseous, dark-grey daylight, the spider of the horizon. But if anything got in Ledin's way while he was traversing one of the deep-buried tunnels between holes and he was in that exaggeratedly poised state of mind, he would calmly order the person to get out of his way through the mine field that surrounded us on all sides. The order had to be obeyed immediately, and the poor victim seldom returned. We were, at the beginning, a company, but now we were no more than twenty men. One after another had had to take the surface route.

I met Ledin in a tunnel when he was in just such a study. I reddened violently and on a kind of childish impulse shouted at him:

"Plennik's taken off for Kámenka! I'm on my way to get him! I know he's there. Anyway, he wouldn't do us any harm. I'm sure of that. But I'd better get on my way in a hurry!"

And Ledin passed me without giving any order. He seemed neither to see me nor to hear me.

Kámenka lay within the mine belt and it was on the way there, along the avenue of horse cadavers, that the animal followed me — if, indeed, it was an animal. My sweat was very salty and froze to sharp crusts in the creases of my skin or ran into my eyes and burned like coals of fire. It was impossible to blink — the eyelids froze together so quickly. Nor could they be dried off with a leather glove frozen as hard as horn. A man couldn't bare his hands even for an instant in such intense cold. The fingers would lose all feeling and act like rubber. It's loathsome to touch anything with fingers like that; the shock can make a man cry or even vomit. In cold like that the eyes burn and hallucinations rise out of the mist. The woods round about become beautiful horses in slow parade or a kind of castle. All very banal, but agreeable. But the crazy little animal that elongated itself or turned into a ball by my side or just behind me — well, I couldn't understand it. Irritated, I jumped impulsively out of the tracks, darted toward the beast, and struck at it with my ski poles. That same moment I got a blow across my face as if from an iron bar. I fell to the ground immediately, with a heavy weight against my chest, and I understood everything at once. It wasn't an animal, but a man. A man in a pure white *arorak* with his skis painted white. Such a man is absolutely invisible against the snow, that is, if he wears white socks over his ski boots. I did, but not this man. As startled and as frightened as I, he fell on me and dug his elbow into my throat. When he did so, I knew he wasn't armed. Out here, nobody went unarmed with one exception: Plennik.

And sure enough it was Plennik! Dressed in the very same white *arorak* that I had recently given him. He was the "animal" — his black feet. Two shoes wandering alone across the deserted surface of the snow, as if in search of their owner. And he was on the way to Kámenka, though he was a miserable skier.

We were both, as it happens, delighted with the meeting and continued together. The lovely horses and the castles — the woods, that is — soon ended, and the path stretched forward across open marshland. At the same time the cold became more savage and more penetrating. In the swamps it's as if some unknown, very light creature jumped up on your back, dug its claws in just below the nape of your neck, blew the marrow out of your upper arms, and filled your leg bones with water from a polar sea. The cold is agonizing.

No more than a kilometer remained to the village, and it occurred to me that no one had told Plennik how it looked now, that there wasn't a single remnant of life, that only chimneys rose, like black towers, above the new snow. Time after time I glanced in the direction of the abandoned shoes that zealously followed me. I wanted to talk, but I couldn't. I knew that his miserable heart burned with longing for Lúnnaja, that his brain worked feverishly, that his frozen lips moved stiffly as he muttered, and that his eyes could already see the image of Lúnnaja. The closer we got to Kámenka, the clearer it became that I hadn't the courage to tell him the truth. And suddenly I began to fear that he would lose his mind at the discovery, fall on me invisibly, and take revenge. I glanced his way, stopped, tried to sharpen my vision to the utmost, but — the abandoned shoes were no longer there.

I listened intensely, but heard nothing. I hurried forward, but there was nothing there. I called out, louder and louder, but no one answered.

I sensed that now I was in the village. It must be village streets that I moved up and down irresolutely while I called out at regular intervals. The anxiety of being abandoned struck at my heart, and sometimes it seemed to me that Plennik must be duping me and that Ledin had a right to his distrust. If such was the case, it would mean that immediately upon my return Ledin would order me to "find a way out." But then again I became fearful that Plennik had only sunk in a heap of misery into the snow and that the cold, which became more heartless by the moment, had already crept into his great nostrils and turned him into a work of art. A dizziness seized me and I quickly put the ski poles in my armpits as supports. I heard the crackling sound of the brittle, white salt crystals around my eyes as I widened them at the sight of something flickering and red. And then I began to argue energetically with myself that the red flicker wasn't merely a fatigue reflex of the optical nerve, but a gleam from far off. I decided to believe that in order to have something to believe, and headed straight for it. Soon I realized that it was, in fact, a glow, perhaps from a small fire. Sometimes it was very weak, like the slow, lingering glimmer in an animal's eye, but other times it was stronger and more yellow.

An overwhelming, naïve gratitude seized me when I got nearer and realized that somebody was indeed starting a fire. And when I recognized that it was Plennik, I wanted to kiss him. He had found his own house, his old home, which lay on the periphery and far from other houses. Only a chimney remained, as was true everywhere else, and all else was leveled to the ground. But the stack was uncommonly broad at the base — and the brick stove around it was intact.

Plennik had hit upon the idea of building a fire in his old stove. When I advanced on him, he neither saw me nor heard me and seemed to be in another world. Like a great, lumbering animal, he nosed his way back and forth through the snow carrying bits of wood and half-charred logs which he dropped into a heap before the stove, one of the old-fashioned Russian type with two great ovens and masonry ledges that a man could crawl up on to warm himself. He brushed all the snow carefully away and after awhile himself clambered up on the stove.

It was clearly useless to attempt to persuade him to follow me back. He was in his home. Somewhat guardedly, I began to help him with the fire. Soon it caught and whistled in the flue, and as the brickwork began to get warm I climbed up and, like Plennik, lay on a ledge on my back.

The northern lights were visible overhead, but they had changed and now divided the sky into two sharply differentiated halves, one light, one dark. Infinity walled the room in which we lay. The arctic cold stood close by and waited, no more than a few inches from our outstretched bodies. It stood with raised axe ready to deliver a lightning blow to the limb that stretched too far out.

Plennik began to speak in a calm, low voice. About us, around the lone stove which stood naked in the middle of the polar night and burned with a roar as if it imagined it could heat up the universe, my friend's narrative conjured up a home. A woman, Lúnnaja, stepped forward and came to life in the red glow from two not quite tight doors in the oven.

She stood on just the spot where she had stood that autumn morning before it was quite light, when Plennik stepped into the house for the first time. He had in his hand that piece of bread, the *prosphorá*, that he had hacked loose from the ice the night before. He was dumbfounded when he stepped in. He had thought they were poor people, poorer than anyone else in the village. He had imagined that the woman for whom the bread was intended suffered from desperate need, but he saw immediately that the circumstances were otherwise. The floorboards were gleaming white, felt boots hung from the ceiling, fur coats and a variety of tools filled every shelf and hook around the walls, and bowls of boiled meat were laid out on the table. An odor of tea and preserves filled the room. On the windowpanes lay the autumn's first snow, which continued to fall in large flakes, confiding and protective.

The woman who stood in the middle of the floor looked to be somewhat over thirty. She simply stood there, alone in the room, illuminated by the dim light from the oven, and sang in a low voice. Feeling a sudden wave of shame at his errand, Plennik quickly stuffed the bread into a pocket. She looked calmly at him and continued to sing, although her voice dropped lower. Her voice was exactly like her, a part of her, and it was rather as if the song clothed her. It was of that soft, fragrant kind that makes a listener become shy in the presence, the all too close presence of her womanliness. Plennik could not bring himself to utter a word, not even a greeting, but stood there with his eyes on the floor. He had a painful sense of his own insignificance and decided to turn around, retreat, flee, disappear, disappear completely from the village for all time and eternity. He had opened the door halfway when he felt a pressure on his arm. The woman held him fast, and when he turned toward her, surprised and a little alarmed, he felt her presence close to him and heard her say abruptly: "Stay here."

Then it was her turn to be surprised at her own conduct. Plennik saw that she was very close to blushing. He became calmer and pulled out the bread, the *prosphorá*, from his pocket. He explained everything but only with his smile, nothing else.

She took the bread, but as she did so something special happened. She could have taken it without touching Plennik's hand. But their hands did touch — unintentionally but unmistakably. She had extended her own hand a little too far, so that when she withdrew it without haste Plennik felt a little caress that made him look quite solemnly straight into her eyes and he noticed that her irises were formed in an unusual way. They were set in her bright eyes like small dark stars, five- or six-pointed stars. She burst into laughter at the solemnity of his manner and he could see all her teeth, even the remotest ones. Her mouth was open that wide. Again he had a sudden desire to rush from the room, but a dry cough from up near the ceiling, or more correctly from the highest ledge on the other side of the stove, brought him back to reason again. A tall man jumped down from up there and the expression on his face made it clear that he owned Lúnnaja, that he was her husband. He had unbelievably long legs and a head that looked a little like the knob on a flagpole. The glow from the oven door made one of his eyes glitter like sunlit dew. It was of glass. As he advanced toward Plennik, it was clear that he was preparing to speak, for the brown mustachios which bristled among the many small wrinkles around his mouth were quivering like the antennae of a wasp. That was, in fact, his name among the villagers, Osa, which means wasp.

40

He explained this after he had joined Plennik, and surprised him by introducing himself as a burgher.

"I'm called the Wasp," he said. "I haven't any idea whether it was my energy and industry that gave me the name or possibly my bad temper. Nobody has ever told me."

He laughed as if he thought he were a very jolly fellow. Then with exaggerated friendliness he invited Plennik to the table by the window where he busied himself preparing tea. All the time he chattered incessantly about the village, its future, the timber cutting, the sawmill, and about himself and how he had worked his way up to *nadsmótrtjik*, or overseer. His mustachios shook and the glass eye, which struck Plennik as being happier and more friendly — indeed more soulful — than the real, slightly scornful eye, glittered all the time. He praised his capable wife and said they had a fifteen-year-old daughter who wrote poetry, and that they were all very happy. After he had finally talked himself out or couldn't think of anything more, he asked Plennik to explain his mission.

By that time it was becoming light outside. Plennik, who sat closest to the window, looked at his hands, which now struck him as particularly dirty and somewhat deformed from the cold. He felt miserable, partly because Osa was clearly a man who had succeeded in life, partly because Lúnnaja could see his own degradation. Consequently he had a desire to insult or frighten his friendly host and hostess, with half a thought that they might drive him from the door. He began to talk about the *prosphorá*, the bread in the ice. He recounted everything in detail, and rather than hide that he intended to kill the man in the dogskin coat, he made a special point of it. When he finished, he twisted around and looked up boldly at the woman who was still standing quietly in the middle of the room.

41

He had expected a hostile look, but what met him was only an expression of anxiety which made her face even more beautiful. Moreover, when he saw that she clutched the miserable piece of bread against her breast, he turned in surprise toward Osa and looked at him. The glass eye was still bland and friendly, but the good eye, now half covered by the lid, was swimming in contempt. However, Osa saved the situation in an instant; he roused himself and said that misfortune could happen to anybody, even the best. And then he laughed disarmingly. After a moment of painful silence the woman said in a low voice:

"It was awfully good of you to risk your life in order to bring me the holy bread."

Plennik didn't need to correct the misinterpretation of the story; Osa did it for him. Osa explained not one time but many, that it was not Plennik who wished to sacrifice himself but the man in the dogskin coat, a former priest of the village whom they all knew. But the woman would not abandon her misunderstanding. Time after time she thanked Plennik, and every time she was corrected by her husband. Finally, angry that she was so obstinately feminine, he stood up with his mustache antennae quivering violently, declared that he had to go to work, and hastened out the door. A moment later he opened it again, stuck in his little head, and, with his glass eye glittering in a friendly fashion, invited Plennik to be his guest until such time as he could find work in the wood.

And so it was. Plennik stayed. He spent the night by the oven, precisely on that ledge where he now lay and told his story. After no more than two days the energetic Osa had arranged work for him. Lúnnaja was to show Plennik the way over the swamp, through the woods, to the timbering locale.

It was a day of deep snow and penetrating sunshine already early in the morning. The sun was still low when they started off, and the granularity of the snow surface created myriads of small, sharp blue shadows that made every square centimeter of snow look like a moon landscape with high mountains. They went very quickly and he carried an axe. She walked ahead of him on the beaten path. He didn't dare look at her, even from behind. She was simply too beautiful and he felt overwhelmed. Uneasily he shifted the axe from one shoulder to the other and tried to keep his eyes on the small moon landscape of the snow crust, but consciousness of her rolling hips in front of him never left him. Suddenly when they were so close to the work area that they could hear every axe blow and also the voices of the woodsmen, she stopped and said quickly:

"I like you. I liked you the minute I saw you."

Her stopping was so unexpected and impulsive that he could not avoid running into her, and they had to grasp each other in order to keep from falling. He was immediately aware of all the softness of her limbs and it made him suddenly brutal. He stepped to the side, sank deep into the snow crust, raised his axe, and thrust the blade into a tree as if he hated it. The spruce branches flew around him and he kicked them with one foot into a pile in the middle of the bright landscape of the snow. It was a place only a few meters from the path, down which anybody might have come walking. She stood quite still and watched with solemn eyes what he was doing.

He smoothed the spruce branches into a bed, put the axe aside, and lifted Lúnnaja up onto the bed. At first she made no resistance, but then she became quite terrified and pointed to the spruce bed in the sunny snow and screamed:

"Look! Look!"

He did not understand. She breathed hard like one who is drowning and gasped as she tried to tear herself away:

"Don't you see what it looks like?"

He now saw that the spruce lay on the snow surface like a newly opened grave. But he only smiled. Nothing could stop him now. He picked her up and put her down on the spruce branches, right in the full sunlight. Axe blows and voices could be heard only a short distance away.

Later they left the bed precisely as it was, without bothering to clear anything away. They went on from there, but not in the direction of the axe blows and voices. Instead they went back home. There they sat waiting for Osa.

CHAPTER 8

CLOUDS
OF HAIL

Now and then, as I sit and talk by the table with the little mimosa on it, I feel as if I were quite alone in the room and merely talking to myself. The delicate chiaroscuro of the spring night has completely obliterated the little mother from my sight, but now and then she reappears quite clearly. Now our relationship seems to be some kind of game, in which the old lady sometimes becomes frightened and withdraws into invisibility. When she dares to come back it is first her eyes that come into view, terribly magnified in the light-darkness, but unfrightened, and in fact challenging:

"Talk on, continue; I know what is ahead and I am prepared for it."

It was just as I arrived at the act of Lúnnaja's adultery

in the sunlit snow that the old lady had been dissolved away and disappeared. I knew very well that it was the thoughtless, approving manner in which I narrated the incident that irritated her and so I pointed out to the old lady what we both very well knew that everywhere and always there are women who "cease their resistance" to men for reasons quite other than love. There are thousands of reasons, both material and highly spiritual — but love needs no reason at all.

Once upon a time Lúnnaja had a reason. It was during the revolutionary years or the time immediately thereafter. She was scarcely more than a child then, and the industrious, enterprising Osa had taken her in his charge and saved her from much misery. He had fought, stolen, and killed for her sake. In a bloody hand encounter he had sacrificed one of his eyes in order to save her life. He would have sacrificed his leg, his arm, and his other eye also if it had been demanded of him. For he worshiped her. That was her attachment to Osa, but it was not enough to withstand love.

On that autumn day when Plennik stepped into Lúnnaja's life, she had lived together with Osa for sixteen years. All those years Osa had gone about and flashed his glass eye and given the impression that marital happiness presided over his house. Lúnnaja had said nothing, but the whole village believed in the happiness of the marriage. She had never deceived him. But she had quietly — and at the beginning quite unconsciously — despised Osa under a cover of gratitude. Certain features and idiosyncrasies of his made her irritable and sometimes even furious: his talkativeness, his quivering mustache, his restless energy. They were the same features and idiosyncrasies some other woman, who might have chosen him, would have loved deeply, deeply as only human beings can love

45

those special characteristics, even failures, in the elect. But also his patience with her, even when she treated him with contempt or indifference, was limitless, this in spite of the fact that as *nadsmótrtjik*, or overseer, he had the reputation of being quick-tempered and spoiling for a fight. He merely smiled, patted her on the arm, and said that she was a little tense. And he condoned her "frigidity" when she thrust him away. But inwardly he despised her because she did not have the intelligence to understand that he was worthy of her love.

On the day that Plennik was to have begun work, Osa walked back and forth impatiently and waited for his wife and Plennik on the timbering location. Every cell of his body was uneasy. Every ten minutes he fished out his big silver watch, flipped open the lid, and stood for a long time with the brown antennae of his mustache quivering. The short day had worn to a close and the sky turned greenish and rose-colored on the horizon. Then he walked back toward the village. As he passed the spruce bed by the path, he stopped abruptly and his whole body stiffened. Even his mustache stood still. His back was quite straight but his one good eye twisted in the direction of the spruce bed. He realized intuitively and without the slightest doubt what had happened.

Once released from his paralysis, he began to run in great strides toward the village and in the direction of his house. Like an elk he came running over the swamp from the edge of the woods. Women standing in their blackened smokehouses became frightened, thinking that an accident had struck some of the workers in the woods. They shouted questions to him, but by that time he had run by without taking any notice at all of their anxiety.

Inside the house the evening light from the windows had already given way to the glow from the oven doors. Lúnnaja and Plennik were sitting silently by the stove

46

when Osa entered. He stopped just inside the door and stiffened again. He stood with a hand on either side of the door, frighteningly like a man crucified, and looked from one of them to the other. His expression was tense as though he were about to commit a criminal act. Lúnnaja returned his look with complete calm. There was not the slightest trace of anguish or doubt in her expression. Plennik, who stood up, was equally calm, but his eyes were full of compassion. Without a word they both confirmed what Osa had suspected, and Osa clearly understood. Not a man or woman in the village who knew Osa would have believed at that instant he would not take revenge. But he did not.

He clearly experienced an infinite disappointment over the absence of any fury in his breast. His expression was drained, leaving only the suspicion of shame over just that emptiness in it. It was as if the deepest, most secret corner of his consciousness already told him that what had happened was what must happen. Then he became confused at his inaction and finally resorted to that emergency expedient men seize upon in the empty, dead moment: he became theatrical. He collapsed in the doorway, grasped at his heart, groaned convulsively, and finally began to whimper like a distressed dog. He remained lying on the floor for some time, shaking now and then as if chilled from head to foot, and beat his fists and forehead against the white floorboards; but at the same time he was unbuttoning his skin vest, button by button, with a good deal of adroitness, easing himself out of it. It was hot in the hut.

Suddenly he jumped to his feet without looking at Lúnnaja or Plennik, gave his vest a kick which carried it far under the bench, and rushed from the house with a fateful finality that suggested that he was going to do violence to himself. But nothing about his behavior frightened Lúnnaja. She looked at Plennik with the same solemn, somewhat questioning tenderness as before.

47

Osa wandered all about the village, from one house to another. Everywhere he described in detail what had happened, and then he asked: "Have I been a good or a bad husband to her?" Everywhere people said to him what was the truth: "A good one, Osa." And then he asked: "Haven't I protected her and given her clothes and jewels?" And they answered: "That you have, Osa." He asked: "Haven't I been sober, hard working, and well behaved?" They said that he had. He asked if he wasn't respected in the eyes of society, and they told him that he was. He asked if he didn't look like a normal human being, and they answered yes, he certainly did. He asked if he had given his wife a healthy daughter, and they nodded. As soon as all his questions were answered, he moved on to the next house and asked the same questions there. And got the same answers. For it was the truth.

While he was out running from house to house, he suddenly thought of the village priest, or, more accurately, the onetime priest, the man in the dogskin coat who was really the source of misfortune in Osa's house. Osa decided to search him out. He nursed a grudge against the priest and had persuaded himself that Father Timofej, as he was called, had brought misfortune upon him as an act of revenge because Osa was an enemy of the church. Osa had contrived to have the church building converted into a community barn for the farmers of the village. In spite of this, Timofej continued to occupy the church; indeed he had established himself in a screened-off area where he had a stove, a straw bed, and an altar. He shored up the fragments of a living, from what people gave him to conduct more or less secret masses, but it was only a few of the oldsters of the village who still came to him. He earned a pittance now and then by attending cows when they calved. Sometimes hunger forced him to work in the woods or in the sawmill, but this happened very seldom. When

48

circumstances became unusually difficult, he would get up at night and stealthily milk some of the village cows. The next day he would go about the village and, with many a hearty laugh, confess that he had been stealing again. But he would never divulge which farmer he had stolen from. The secret belonged to him, the cow, and to God, he would say.

He was a very handsome, dark-skinned man with shining white teeth, a man who carried his tall, slim figure gracefully, but in no disturbingly feminine way. He was accustomed to wear his dogskin coat almost the year around. The priestly knot of hair on the nape of his neck was always half undone and hung in black tufts down his back. On his head he wore a wool cap that he himself had knitted and decorated with a little cross that stood out in relief. He moved his large, handsome hands with much grace when he spoke, and he spoke a good deal without being urged, always with a delighted expression on his face which seemed to say: "What a lot of rubbish I can toss off! And why shouldn't I toss off a lot of rubbish?"

When Osa stepped into Father Timofej's dwelling, amid the lowing and the odor of cattle, he found the priest on his knees in prayer, illuminated by the glow from a pitch brand. Timofej knelt before a house altar which he himself without any great talent had fashioned. The icons on the wall consisted of yellowed newspaper clippings, some in color, and a piece of wood was bent into the form of an arch within which hung a bell. It was a chapel bell. When Father Timofej finished, he brushed the straw from his knees, looked up at Osa, and said laughingly:

"Look at my little chapel! Have you seen the like of it? What a chapel! Go ahead and laugh at it Osa, if you like. It doesn't bother me in the least."

And since he laughed in such an open, hearty fashion, Osa himself had to smile. Then Timofej became serious:

"The person praying and the person prayed to are in fact one and the same. Don't you know that? It was common knowledge as early as the Greeks."

But Osa had already begun to tell what had happened at his house, and he did it in a tone of voice that suggested that Timofej was responsible. After he had asked all the questions and they had, in turn, been answered by Timofej as they had been by all the other villagers, Osa said in an aggrieved tone of voice:

"You will admit that I was always a good husband?"

Timofej, who had been sitting on a pile of straw on the floor, stood up slowly and said, with his dark eyes quite wide:

"What's that got to do with love? Love is something entirely separate! Don't you understand that?"

After a short pause he added thoughtfully, as he resumed his seat on the pile of straw:

"What a sweet idiot you are!"

This was too much for Osa. After all he was a *nadsmótrtjik*, and so he hastened from the priest's house, his face grey and his mustaches violently quivering.

Osa returned to his own house quite late that night. Plennik had gathered together his meager belongings and dressed himself with the intention of spending the night in some outbuilding. Lúnnaja had not succeeded in persuading him to stay. Just as Plennik reached the hall, Osa strode in and pulled him back into the living room. Osa had changed his demeanor; he had decided to be magnanimous. He insisted that Plennik continue to live in the house, and assured him that he would not have it otherwise. He went about preparing tea and showed both Plennik and Lúnnaja the greatest politeness. He bowed with a certain formality when he said goodnight and retired to sleep on the uppermost oven ledge with his clothes on, indicating that Plennik should take over the place at

Lúnnaja's side in the little bedroom. But instead Plennik went down to the sawmill and spent the night there. The following day Osa insisted that Plennik stay on at the sawmill, which was located in the village proper, and he gave him a good job so that "he wouldn't be separated too far from Lúnnaja."

Before the villagers Osa gave the impression of a broken man, very urbane and mannerly, but rapidly wasting away. Sometimes he squeezed out his glass eye with his thumb, stuck it in a trouser pocket, and went around with the socket empty as if to show his complete indifference to everything. But the villagers had no special sympathy for Osa and his fate. At first this astonished him, and after a short time he began to hate them in silence. But most of all he hated the village priest, Timofej, whom he looked upon as an abscess. One day while Timofej was working in the sawmill and stood in the neighborhood of the big crosscut blade, Osa thrust himself in front of him and stood there staring contemptuously at him without saying a word. But Timofej spoke. He showed all his white teeth and shouted above the buzzing saw blade:

"There's a whole lot you can't understand in life, Osa, but one thing is sure. When your wife deceived you, it was in some curious way the will of God."

Osa's face turned white, and like lightning he grabbed a heavy stick from the floor and raised his long arm as if to strike. But the movement was too violent. Because his blind eye was on the side toward the saw blade, he did not realize he had come so close. The blade caught his leather jacket, jerked him to the saw table, and pulled him in. Before anyone could turn off the machine, the accident had happened. The saw blade had cut into his waist and very nearly divided him in two. His death was instantaneous and free of pain.

Timofej hastened immediately to Lúnnaja's house. He

51

ran in his heavy coat, and people who did not suspect the nature of the errand laughed at him because all the curs of Kámenka were at his heels, yapping and excited by the smell of the coat. But he was used to dogs and paid no attention to them.

Inside Lúnnaja's house, Timofej advanced without hesitation to the woman who stood in the thin rose-colored firelight in the middle of the floor and gently took her hand in both of his, without saying a word. He had always been very warmly attached to Lúnnaja. But she pulled her hand away energetically, as if his approach had been all too intimate. He looked up in surprise. Even though he was unable to see that it was not Lúnnaja, he now realized that it was, instead, her and Osa's daughter, the fifteen-year-old Elisa, who was outwardly very much like her mother, if a trifle larger, in spite of her youth, and more robust.

She was a mature girl or, more correctly, a woman, this Elisa, whom no one understood. She seemed contemptuous of everything and everybody, had no inclination to take any kind of job, and was secretly referred to by the villagers as the Princess. She associated with no one, paid not the slightest heed to the other young people, for the most part stayed in her room, lay in her bed, and read. It was generally known that she had the same beautiful voice as her mother, but no one had had the chance to hear her sing. She seemed to be a dreamer, although no one had any idea what she dreamt about. But she had a sharp mind and people were in general afraid of her. What kind of poetry she wrote, they had not the slightest idea.

As soon as Timofej had carried out his mission and described the accident down in the sawmill, Elisa rushed from the room, and went into her bedroom, slammed the door, and locked it. Timofej knocked but she refused to open. He listened and heard no sound from within.

He waited for quite some time, but no one came. Then he went down into the village in order to seek out Lúnnaja.

During the following days Father Timofej was seen to go many times to Osa's house. He was summoned there — not by Lúnnaja, but by Elisa. They talked in her bedroom. That is to say, she did all the talking, compulsively without pause, while he listened. She wanted a church burial for her father and she got her wish, even though Timofej was most hesitant and considered that Osa himself would never have wished any such thing and that it would only anger the people of the village. The last argument made Elisa completely unshakable in her intent.

It was still autumn and the first snow had come and gone. That day when *Nadsmótrtjik* Osa was to be conducted to his last rest, Elisa had hung white sheets over all the mirrors in the house and arranged for Father Timofej to read prayers and administer extreme unction. She would not let her mother approach the dead man without carrying lighted candles in her hands. She had also obtained some yellow sand to strew over her father's remains before he was carried on a flat wagon to the church, where they could not enter but where Timofej lifted out his little home-made chapel and set it up against the church wall. The whole village was there to observe the spectacle, as they called it, and Elisa behind her veil acted as if the reactions of the simple folk were hardly worth taking any notice of at all. And the people even yielded to her firmness of will and formed, somewhat self-consciously, an old-fashioned funeral procession. Father Timofej came first, but without his dogskin coat because Elisa had forbidden it, and so he was shaking with cold in the icy blasts and showers of hail. He held an icon high in one hand, he shook a thurible in the other, and he sang in full voice. A coachman led the horse by its bridle and on the carriage rested the coffin with the lid up so that Osa's sharp, white profile was outlined against the lead-grey sky. On his head was a "little crown," a band of paper covered with Bible quotations and interspersed with small, naïve images of saints, which Timofej had himself somewhat awkwardly fashioned. When the cortege arrived at the sawmill, the scene of the accident, it stopped a moment and Timofej's clear voice rang out:

"God have mercy! Holy God, powerful God, infinite and eternal God, have mercy!"

After the procession had advanced partway across the swampland toward the burial place, torrents of hail began to fall, rattling with a dry sound on *Nadsmótrtjik* Osa's forehead, eyebrows, and lips, and rebounding in wide arcs over the two women who walked next to the funeral carriage. Elisa walked very erect with her head held high, defying her father's authority and feelings to the last. She was the fruit of a marriage where lovelessness had made the atmosphere sterile and oppressive.

Lúnnaja walked by her side, silent and indistinguishable in the procession. Naïvely, innocently, and quite illogically she was grateful to that providence which, at the moment when sorrow struck, brought Plennik into her life.

CHAPTER 9

THE EVENING
OF THE
GREEN INSECTS

When ice-laden fuel is thrown into a burning stove, great clouds of steam rush up through the smoke outlet and rise into the cold above in the form of high, gently rolling white marble pillars that grow and spread with great rapidity. But then, after the water has been tormented out of the wood and it burns dryly, there remains only a turbulence of air, full of small soot particles, over the mouth of the smoke hole, and the glow of the fire illuminates those millions of small soot particles and makes the hot air around the chimney opening shine like a little sunset.

I lay there on the oven ledge, staring up at the little sunset which alternately increased and subsided in intensity, and listened to Plennik as he continued to talk, but in quite a different way from his former manner. He interrupted his narrative frequently, took long pauses, and then resumed a sentence he had begun earlier. I understood that his account was about to reach that time which was sacred to him, the great happiness of his love for Lúnnaja. It seemed that he and Lúnnaja lived openly together in her house and that he assumed a foreman's job at the sawmill. Elisa continued to grow but without losing any of her mother's beauty of contour and countenance, and at five o'clock every morning she made her way to Father Timofej with whom she glutted herself on masses, sacraments, confessions, fasts, and everything that the old hated church had to offer. She walked through the village in a manner which intimated that religion was something people did not have enough intelligence and education to appreciate, and it was as if she enjoyed defying the ideology of a whole continent now that her father was no longer living to oppose her. She continued to write poetry but nobody other than Timofej was considered worthy to read it.

Then when Plennik began to describe Elisa's indolence and her condescension toward Lúnnaja, his voice failed him time after time. For long intervals he was quite silent, and I did not wish to disturb him. But suddenly — I don't quite know why — I got the feeling of being alone where

I lay. I raised myself to a sitting position and noticed that the stove wall had suddenly cooled off, and I called out immediately:

"Plennik where are you?"

I got no answer. Anxiously I groped around the place where Plennik had been lying. It was empty. He had vanished in his usual, imperceptible way. I jumped down, broke off some bits of plank, and threw them hastily into the stove. Then I called out again, but in vain. I pulled out a piece of burning wood and by its light soon discovered footprints in the snow leading straight out across the swamp. The snow creaked and complained under my feet as I followed the tracks at a half run. Scarcely fifty meters away, I found Plennik. In the light of my burning torch I could see that he stood quite still and that he had pulled off the wool rags wrapped around his head and thereby bared his ears. He gesticulated at me with his arms.

"Quiet," he whispered. "For God's sake don't make so much noise!"

"What is it?" I whispered back.

He did not answer immediately. He just stood there, tense, and then raised his arm and pointed in the direction of the forest edge and the beginning of the mine field. It then occurred to me that our fire was a thoughtless act and that the "sunset" around the chimney must have shown a long way off. We did not know what lay beyond the mine field, and my first impulse was to run back and put out the fire. But Plennik caught me by the arm.

"Don't you hear anything?" he hissed.

I tramped out the burning brand in the snow, bared my ears, and strained my hearing to the utmost but detected nothing. He repeated his question, and I noticed that his voice was shaking.

"No," I said, "nothing."

"Not now," he said, "but a few minutes ago."

"Heard what?" I drew back a step when he answered: "Lúnnaja."

I was quite stunned by his answer, but he said calmly, as if he had read my thoughts:

"No, I'm not imagining things. I'm not losing my mind. I heard her. She was singing. Over there, a long way off."

He pointed into the distance. I could not see what he was pointing at, but I could hear something. While we had been lying in the heat of the stove, the moisture had been forced out of our clothes and *anoraks*. This moisture, once out in the cold again, instantly froze to ice and at every movement our clothes crackled and creaked with a noise much like that a man makes walking over a heap of twigs.

I felt a nervous prickling sensation at the roots of my hair, and said immediately in a purposely ordinary tone of voice, as if to put all fantasies to flight:

"The fact is, my dear friend, on your side it often happens, very often, that there are women in the lines, even in the front lines, and I've heard singing out in the woods before, very pretty and talented singing, but just now . . ."

"It was she," he interrupted. He was breathing with difficulty, like a man drowning.

"Well," I said, "even if you did hear a woman's voice singing somewhere in the distance, which I doubt, it isn't necessarily your particular woman. You know that."

"I recognize the song," he answered abruptly. "It was a song of our own, a song that we made up ourselves. About the *prosphorá*, that little piece of bread."

"There are many who could have learned it," I said, in an effort to calm him. "And moreover," I added, with an attempt at an understanding laugh, "I can assure you that there is absolutely nothing, neither . . ."

"I can hear better than you, you know that," he said in a stern voice.

A moment later my ear caught the sound of his arm moving in an admonition for complete silence.

I listened. And then I too heard something, infinitely far off. But it was not singing. Sometimes it was motors, and mixed up with the sound of motors, the neighing of horses. One time I heard three or four hammer blows against metal. But then it came — a high, sustained, and then slowly sinking sound from a woman's throat. Faintly, like the whine of insect wings high in the air. And then it was silent again.

"This time you heard it," he said.

"No," I answered. "Nothing more than a motor, possibly, a long way from here. It's just that you are upset and exhausted . . ."

Then he lost his temper. For the first time Plennik's voice sounded hard and charged with anger.

"Don't stand there lying," he shouted at me.

I answered as quickly and abruptly, with a kind of cold, curt decisiveness:

"No. And if you heard singing, it was pure hallucination!"

I lied and I was forced to it. I had to convince him, even with an untruth. Otherwise nothing would have held him back. He would have gone straight out into the mine field, straight as an arrow toward his objective.

For one moment my determination faltered. A second later I thanked God that it was pitch black around us and that he could not see the doubt that was certainly mirrored in my face. I had thought: "Why not let him go?" But then the instinct for self-preservation asserted itself: if I returned to Ledin without Plennik, I would instantly be sent out to "find a way." And I became that much more firm in my decision to convince Plennik.

"Now we'll go back to the stove, warm up for a while, and then head for home again. We've been away far too long. It's not good." As soon as I finished talking, I started abruptly. It was the woman's voice again. No nearer, but stronger than before. And my innermost thought was: "That is precisely the way I had imagined Lúnnaja's voice."

"Let's go," I said.

"You must have heard!" he said, his voice full of dismay.

"Heard what?"

I sensed that he was both confused and embarrassed by the assurance in my voice. He must have depended a very great deal on me. I heard his breathing become more and more vehement. Like a child just before he begins to cry. He stood stock-still a moment, while the singing faded away.

"If there isn't anything," he said in a voice that was more lifeless than before, "then . . . then I must be sick."

"No," I answered, "not sick. But tired. Exhausted, body and soul. We all are. And it sometimes happens to all of us that we think we make contact with that which we love the most."

I moved slowly back toward the stove while I continued to talk to him, and to my surprise I sensed that he was following me. I had not thought he would accept my deceit so easily. And the fact was that he had not. When we reached the stove, I discovered that it was not on my account that he had followed. He immediately set about breaking up more fuel with an energy and strength that I did not believe he possessed. He fired the stove again with passionate zeal. Before he threw the wood into the fire, he scraped it free of ice and snow with a precision and pedantry that must mean something. It meant that he wanted to create a shining "sunset," so that whoever was

59

on the other side of the mine field would note the fire, become curious, and come toward it. From time to time he cast a sidelong glance at me with eyes which were serious and anxious in such a doglike way. He wanted to see whether I saw through his trick, and I couldn't withhold a laugh. Then I said:

"My dear friend, why is it so desperately important that you see this woman? She'll wait for you. You live in each other's hearts."

He interrupted his work for a moment and looked thoughtful.

"Perhaps we do, yes. And perhaps not. You can't be sure. That's what is so hard to bear — the uncertainty."

Suddenly he looked up into my eyes and said:

"The green insects. Do you know them?"

I did not understand the question, but he continued anyway:

"You know how it is during grenade fire. You root down in the snow and lie still. Dig with your hands, feet, knees, and shoulders, yes, even with your head. Deeper and deeper down. There you lie still. Then comes the exhaustion that is harder to combat than the grenades, because it is so lovely. You lie there and kick happiness away. But you know what I am telling you. Then the insects come flying. Green insects come dancing through the air and strike hard all over the face and the nape of the neck. Hundreds of pine needles broken off and violently agitated by the blasts. They strike hard against your skin and sometimes stick to you, if you are smeared with grease. They wake you up. They save you from the sleep in the snow from which a man never wakes up. You want to kiss them afterwards, those small green insects. But you know all this. Well, one evening I distinguished something in the snow in front of me, something that looked a little darker than anything around it — like a hole. The grenades were falling and I threw myself at what I thought was a hole. But it was no hole; it was a man, a soldier. He had just fallen asleep, and the insects had no effect on him because he had pulled all his wool rags and his *anorak* down over his face. You know what a fool he was! He woke up when I fell on him and he did not have enough sense to be thankful. Instead he became angry and growled at me. I recognized his voice immediately; it was a man from my own village, Kámenka, and he had just arrived at the front. It was, in fact, the same man with the red, bushy beard who once pulled me out of the river when I was floating around with the ice and the bread. He was a good man, but a fool. He was so tired that I had to force him to talk, talk, and talk, to prevent sleep from seizing him. What he said, what I drew out of him, saved me also from going to sleep. He said things that made me wide awake. You might say that his words saved me from freezing, but they froze my heart. They were painful words.

"What he said — Redbeard, that is — was that one time, just before the war broke out, he made his way to the church in Kámenka, the church that was a barn, and lay down in the straw. He owned a cow that he thought was going to calve in the night. As it happens, he lay down close to the thin board walls with which Father Timofej screened off his living quarters. The cow didn't calve; Redbeard lay there till morning; and when it was five o'clock, Timofej had a visitor. It was Elisa. Timofej first conducted his morning mass, and then he chatted with Elisa. It was as if she were confessing to Father Timofej. Neither of them had any idea that Redbeard lay nearby and heard every word."

Plennik had already suspected for some time that Elisa was infatuated with Timofej, and Redbeard verified his suspicions. Elisa wasn't the only one; all the women and girls of the village worshiped him as a man and made light of him as a priest. Timofej was very much aware of all this, but he merely dismissed the matter with a laugh. He was partly flattered and partly annoyed.

Elisa was a remarkable girl; she had her own way of meeting life. Redbeard had not recognized her voice at all, so different was it when she was with Father Timofej. She, who did not weep a single tear over her father's death, now talked like a martyr, like a saint. Her voice, otherwise so cold and condescending, was full of nuances now — warm, captivating, and human. She suffered, you could tell. She was defenseless, she felt herself hunted "like a hind in the woods," she said. The danger that threatened her could be pinpointed; it was "the guest in the house," Plennik. He had loved her passionately for more than a year, she lied to Father Timofej. His hunger for her was boundless — and she suffered. She would not deny that she felt a warm sympathy for his quiet, gently refined bearing, but she could not return his love. He came to her at night, while Lúnnaja was asleep, and begged and beseeched her. She was in continuous anguish that some day he would take his own life. She felt a great, overwhelming sympathy for him. She went into some detail and told how she had unexpectedly come upon him one midnight during the summer, when the sun had not succeeded in reaching below the horizon but rested like an inflamed sore against the pale yellow sky, plaguing people into sleeplessness. Plennik had stolen out of the house to her clothes which were hanging on the line, laid them upon the ground, and was smothering them with kisses. Another night during the same summer, Elisa continued, he went down to the river after Elisa had repulsed him. She had become frightened and followed at a distance. He had removed his clothes and swum back and forth, back and forth, apparently with the sole intent of exhausting himself. When he came too close to a stand of weeds, he had become helplessly entangled in the soft, slimy growth, and was unable to tear himself loose. He was unconscious by the time Elisa had thrown herself into the water and pulled him out, but she saw that he was breathing faintly. Then she had run away from him, she said, so that he would not know who it was that saved him. But she had been there long enough to see his naked body, to see how handsome he was and how powerfully built. Yet she had no feeling for him.

Elisa continued to lie to Timofej. Detail after detail. Redbeard lay and listened. He came back the next day to listen. He brought other villagers with him, curious young boys and girls. They all had a chance to listen, and the whole village began to whisper and gossip.

One time, when Elisa had forced herself physically on Timofej, he became very angry and shouted so that it echoed in the old cow-smelling sanctuary:

"No! You have to love *mankind* in order to be able to love *one* man! And you can't!"

There were those who sympathized with Plennik, for Elisa was very lovely indeed.

When the war came, Plennik, Timofej, and Elisa all found themselves at the front — two soldiers and a nurse — and all of those left behind in the village did much talking. The rumor of this tragic, secret love reached Lúnnaja's ears. Just how she took this blow against her heart Redbeard could not tell Plennik. He said he didn't know.

By the time he finished his account, Plennik's whole body was shaking, and I shall never forget the fear in his clear eyes when he looked at me. It was as if his lips did not have the courage to question me:

"Can justice be done? And can the infernal lies of a neurotic be wiped out? Is the truth really stronger than the neurosis?"

I do not remember how I consoled him, but I do recall that a moment later he realized that he had neglected the fire. He sprang into action, digging for scraps of wood among the charred remains. Suddenly his attention was caught by something dark in what had once been a floor. It was the passage down to a little cellar. He took a burning stick of wood and clambered down. I walked over and looked at him from above. He illuminated all the indefinable objects below and seemed to be looking purposefully for something. I asked him what it was, but he did not bother to answer. Then he crouched down, stuck the torch in the ground near him, and reached out after something. It was a small, square iron box. He then clambered up again with the box in his arms. I wanted to help him with his burden, but he would not let me. He set the iron box down in the light of the stove, looked at it for a long time, and finally opened it.

"O God," I heard him mumble. "O God, O God."

I stepped forward and looked. The box was completely empty. As tactfully as possible I asked him what he had expected to find in the little box.

"The bread," he answered. "The *prosphorá.*"

They had always kept it in the box, he explained. And yet I could not understand why a somewhat childishly beatific expression came over his face, and he approached me as if he wished to embrace me. Then he said in a loud voice, almost shouting:

"She took it with her! She took the bread with her when she left the village! That means she still thinks of me! And believes in me! Otherwise she would not have taken it with her!"

His confidence and joy grew stronger by the minute and he seemed to forget every other thing in the world. I took advantage of the opportunity to issue orders for departure.

64

He obeyed. His state was such that he said to me: "I'll do anything you like. Just command!"

And so we set out from there.

CHAPTER 10

SOMEONE
WALKS AMONG
THE DEAD

Two days later the Russians had discovered us in our patch of woods. Catastrophe crept nearer.

When it happened I was standing watch. I was standing by the edge of our old defenses, near a configuration of abandoned trenches which we had used while we were still a company. A little glade lay immediately before me. The memory of dead comrades lived on in the empty trenches, and loneliness and cowardice welled up within me. The darkness was suddenly rent asunder with incomprehensible heartlessness, as a flare began its descent.

A flare is cataclysmic. It is impossible to say exactly where it comes from — only that it comes from the enemy side. It flames up for a time over the treetops, cuts a great gash of light in the polar night, and descends with sadistic leisure. The white light of the rocket is, like the enemy division's hostility, concentrated in an inaccessible, sinking, hissing, and spitting little ball of fire in the air. A forest that has been in continuous darkness for so long that even the chlorophyll of the trees seems to have turned black should not be surprised in such a fashion! Even the darkness itself seems to be seized by a burning pain when it is ripped apart.

I was standing alone in the woods when it happened. The light flamed up just above and in front of me, spraying my insignificance with its unnatural intensity as if I were a piece of scenery in an opera set. It was as if I were suddenly stripped, as if the light penetrated my clothes, and as if a million enemy eyes laughed at me from all of the oppressive darkness outside the circle of light. Eyes that could clearly see my very intestines, like those of fish spawn, that could clearly discern my miserable terror and my comic harmlessness in spite of weapons: "So you were standing here, little friend, guarding the earth in the middle of the night!"

From the moment that a flare is ignited in one's vicinity until it hisses into the snow like an angry animal, wounded to the death, the process of thought stops quite still. The time continuum is no longer segmented and therefore becomes an infinity. It illuminates not merely the physical man, but the deepest secrets close to a man's heart at the moment of surprise. In the heartless light it was as if I could see myself and my fantasies — namely, that a young girl, Elisa, was walking in the snow. After several hours of guard duty, everything, even the merest suspicion of light, begins to live, move, walk, or run. Elisa was just as Plennik had described her. She was buxom and radiantly lovely with scornful eyes. She walked most gracefully among the dead, the frozen, lying here in the snow, not like men, but like so many artifacts. Sometimes she looked at them, it seemed to me, but quite unmoved, cold, and almost with a certain satisfaction. It is admittedly not a frightening sight. The dead have intricate and "happy" positions, as if they had stiffened just at the moment of cycling to the neighborhood store with a child on the handlebars or while they were bent backward in the steambath, beating their chests with fresh birch branches, or while they played the violin, perched on a fence some festive evening. So they looked, as if they lay reaching into the air after invisible instruments. Or played on invisible instruments. And Elisa walked among them and honored them from time to time by listening. Finally I was struck by an irresistible desire to raise my automatic pistol, take aim at her, and say:

"It's you, and your brothers and sisters, who shape catastrophe everywhere, the large and the small. Because you love catastrophe and need it as well — you ask a sound thrashing of life itself — and you are going to get it. It is you and those like you who so carefully and seductively conjure up war, the greatest of catastrophes. You have power. You are strong. People are afraid of you. Sometimes they follow you, because each and every one has a germ of neurosis, born out of lovelessness. If it were not so, we would be gods . . ."

That was my vision.

It was only when the flare had extinguished itself deep in the snow and the darkness was healed again that I came to and it became entirely clear to me what the flare meant. As though with its own hissing voice it had greeted me:

"Thanks for the 'sunset' the other night! That's what attracted us here. And now we know where you are!"

I hastened with the greatest speed to Ledin in order to report the flare. I thought, as I ran, that there was, in any event, something safe, realistic, and reliable about that man.

CHAPTER 11

THE STRUGGLE
THAT WILL
NOT BE PART
OF HISTORY

While Tom sat cleaning the carbide lamp — really the only thing he ever did with sure success — I described everything that had happened during Plennik's and my visit in Kámenka. Tom brightened up in a way that was quite unusual for him, but then he loved Plennik as much as I did, and we both knew that we should in secret do all we could to smuggle Plennik back to his own people again, in spite of Ledin and his view of the affair. While others talked, Tom usually sat in solemn silence, fingering the bumpy fat on his dark, dirty brow; but this time a burning light appeared in his eyes and he said that once at the beginning of the war he had heard the voice of a woman singing from the enemy lines and that there had been an intense burst of gunfire in the middle of the song, just as if the song had been arranged in order to lull and mesmerize his side at the moment of attack. Ledin and the Bouncer had also been along that time, Tom said, and he begged me with almost childish eagerness not to say anything to them about Lúnnaja's song. They would be even less sympathetic with Lúnnaja and Plennik then, Tom argued.

I did not take his story very seriously. It was so typical of him: emotional, unrealistic, and a little childish. But, in any case, it was precisely the unrealistic and the somewhat childish that happened to us the very evening after Tom had told his story.

A woman sang. We heard it as clearly as if we had been in a concert hall. She sang in such a characteristically feminine way that a man who heard it would inevitably be a little distraught. The voice painted such a beautiful picture of the woman herself. I could catch every word of the song. It was a tender and somewhat sentimental song about love, and a word that was repeated was *prosphorá*, or "the bread of love." In the middle of the song came the attack, like a whining hailstorm of steel.

One hour before it happened we all lay crowded together under the carbide lamp in the hole — Ledin, Plen-

68

nik, Tom, and I. Only the Bouncer was out. The temperature had stayed between 20 and 25 degrees below all day, and there was some wind. We lay quite still, knotted together, intricated in each other's limbs, like a mass of baby snakes. The only thing we could move, without the risk of disturbing and angering the next man, was the head — precisely as with baby snakes. When a head sometimes raised itself carefully and cautiously from the human heap, it was always with the sole purpose of looking at that square iron box, the stove. We wanted sleep but got none. Thirst kept us wide awake. We lay there and suffered. Something was dying down there — namely, the fire. There was no more fuel for it.

All the dry spruce wood in our vicinity had been collected and burned. There was no more to be had. Nor could we range any further from our camp, according to Ledin's order. No one could leave the immediate vicinity after the incident of the flare. The enemy was everywhere in the woods. The mine field was theirs, and it was no hindrance to them because they had mapped it. They were looking for us. These last days we had heard them every hour. There were thousands of them. We merely lay there squeezed into our holes, and were entrenched even to the extent of having pulled in our sentries from outer positions. The wind had helped us by wiping out all trace of paths and tracks around us. All weapons had been removed to the holes, in spite of the danger of rust.

On the stove there were small steel cups, or canteen lids, filled with snow. The heat should have melted the snow down and turned it to water, but the stove cheated us.

Even if melted snow is not water but a tasteless liquid without salts, and even if a whole cupful of snow is reduced to no more than a spoonful of a tasteless liquid, nevertheless it was a painful longing for just that spoonful that

69

drove sleep from us. We lay there and listened. The snow in the cups changed no longer. There had been some movement only moments ago, a trace of a movement, a contracting, the snow becoming more granular and dark, as if it had broiled and subsided with a sigh. We lay there and waited for several more sighs. The cold from the forest above penetrated down to us even more insolently. The little stick of light in the carbide lamp crept in terror back into the lamp but the sighs came no longer. The stove was exhausted. The snow lay motionless and dead.

The snow's last evanescent sigh lingered in our ears. Occasionally some one of us would think that he could hear it so clearly that life returned to his eyes and he raised his earth-smeared head and looked in the direction of the cups or toward the cardboard door in the ceiling. The Bouncer also sighed, when he was around, and it sounded much the same. We waited for him too. For once we actually wanted him there with us. He had Ledin's permission to search for wood. He had picked up the axe and said:

"I haven't any doubt that fuel's to be found hereabouts. If a man has his eyes about him. You can't be at such a loss . . ."

He maintained that from the position where he last stood watch he had seen a large, grey, almost whitened, dry pine some distance in the woods. He had had his eye on it for quite a while now, he said. But it lay in dangerous territory, he said. It wasn't precisely child's play to fetch it out of a wood full of "big game." But he had walked off in great strides, wearing an expression as if to say that it was always he who in the hour of need came to the rescue of us helpless creatures.

We had no idea how long it had been that we lay waiting for him. The cold was so intense that even our watches moved only by fits and starts. I was the first to lose patience, and I jumped up from the spruce branches on the floor.

"If that stupid cod is seeing sights as he usually does, I'll be happy enough if he gets the axe back here!" I shouted: "Then I'll go out and split the whole damned world. And burn up . . ."

As if in immediate answer, the roof door opened and the Bouncer clambered in. The stubble of his beard was chalk-white with frost, even into his nostrils. We looked up at his neck which was round and red like a storm sun against all that white. He did not display any special humility, so he must have found wood! He must have found dry pine! Ledin immediately lit a cigarette. Tom began to speak in a voice that already anticipated water in the steel cups on the stove.

"Have you got wood outside?" he said. "Have you a lot of wood? Did you find the pine tree?"

"Hurry up and throw in a little wood," I snapped. "Stop stalling. Why didn't you bring in a couple of sticks right away?"

The Bouncer made no move to go out and bring in wood. He stood there in his black coat, looming large and self-important, with the hood of the *anorak* pulled down so that his eyes could not be seen. But he did not act contrite and he did not sigh. Suddenly he said:

"I haven't got any wood . . ."

We remained motionless. Thirst flamed up with renewed strength and our voices became hollow.

"You were seeing things as usual?" I said.

"No," he answered, and his voice was defiantly calm. But he did not raise the *anorak* hood to meet my eyes.

"That's just what I didn't," he continued. "The pine tree *is* there."

71

"You didn't think it advisable to go that far?" said Ledin. "There was enemy around?"

"I was there, Ledin," he answered swiftly. "Believe me, I was there."

"Were you too lazy to chop?" Tom wondered.

"I chopped," said the Bouncer.

"And so you came home," I said sarcastically, "and let the pine tree lie there? So the 'big game' would have something to broil itself upon?"

"No," answered the Bouncer. "Don't you understand that I had to chop as rapidly as possible, so those in the vicinity would have no chance to discover where the axe blows came from. For then they'd naturally open fire. Don't you understand that?"

"Understand!" I burst out and grabbed him by the neck, whereupon the hood fell further down and hid his whole face except for the chin and mouth. He made no move to shift the hood.

"I had to hurry," he said in a somewhat more nervous tone of voice. "I had to and so I went at it as hard as I could . . ."

"Well?"

"The snow was a meter deep around me. It had been blown into drifts up there."

"Well?"

"In cold as terrible as that, even steel changes its character . . ."

"Well — l?"

"And so . . . with all that strength . . . with the power the blow carried . . . the axe head flew off the handle."

My hand opened and released its grip on the Bouncer's neck. My comrades shut their eyes. Now all hope was gone. We all knew that an axe head which has shot off the handle and disappeared into the snow is not likely to be found

72

again. However systematically and logically you search, and however long, you never find it. An axe head does not reveal itself until the snow melts in the spring.

If the Bouncer had retreated to his customary place and sat on his haunches as he used to do when he was embarrassed or if he had delivered himself of a single sigh as snow does when it melts, then we would have lapsed into silence and motionlessness on our hole's spruce floor. But he said:

"Well, you don't need to look so damned down-in-the mouth. You ought to be able to take . . ."

Then something happened that left Ledin, Plennik, and me staring in astonishment. Tom, the gentle and good-natured Tom, jumped up from his place and struck the Bouncer full in the face. It was as if his fist flew out of its own accord, and he seemed just as surprised as any of the rest of us. The Bouncer was completely silenced. You could not even hear his breathing. He did not move or even bother to raise the hood of his *anorak*. All we could see was his mouth. Only seconds after the blow, his upper lip began to swell up, giving him a comical appearance, and Tom, who had resumed his place on the floor, stared in fright at the transformation he had caused. In spite of this, a strange smile spread on the Bouncer's face under the thickening upper lip, and we observed him with something approaching anxiety. Ledin removed his cigarette from his mouth, lifted his eyebrows, and fixed his gaze on the Bouncer's peculiar mouth.

We all understood that the Bouncer was about to outdo himself and that he had some kind of trump card which he had not yet played. Suddenly he struck the hood of the *anorak* from his face. His brown eyes observed us for a moment as if he were some kind of overseer, whereupon he began to talk to Ledin as if the two were alone together in the hold. He explained that while he was creeping about in the snow searching for the axe head, he made a discovery, a very important discovery. He came upon an enemy machine gun nest, he said. He had wriggled up to it and in the weak light from the snow he had seen it clearly, very clearly, indeed. It looked like a great, grey face, he said. It was as if it had eyes and a broad mouth and a long nose — the muzzle. Just like a face, he assured us.

Ledin said that there was nothing to do about it just now, but the Bouncer argued that there was. An automatic weapon was precisely what we were going to need. Those who manned it ought to be disposed of silently with bayonets, so that no one should hear and come to their rescue. Ledin pondered over the matter for a while, then turned to Tom and me, and asked if we would accompany the Bouncer on the mission.

"No," answered Tom bluntly, without looking up from where he lay.

I asked Ledin in a calm voice, ignoring the Bouncer's presence, if Ledin couldn't yet see through the Bouncer, that everything he got involved in went awry and brought more trouble in its wake. Wasn't it simply that the Bouncer had a compulsion to prove himself? But this was no beer joint, where the Bouncer could throw people out according to his pleasure.

The Bouncer stood there tightening his bayonet while he observed me with pity. I lay down next to Tom. We were no heroes, Tom and I. For a time there was silence down in the hole, and the wind could be heard intensifying up in the woods. One of us kept shifting about, quite unnecessarily — the Bouncer.

"I'm going to go," he said. "And get it over with."

He talked as if he had a harelip. The fact was that his upper lip jutted out from his face, thick and stiff.

"I'm going. Alone. Since . . ."

74

That little word, that last word, that "since" he uttered in a way that caused even Ledin to start.

For a long time after he had gone, the memory of his swollen upper lip lingered in our little hole. Tom lay there sighing from time to time in a deep and troubled fashion, like an old horse, and we understood that he regretted the blow and was having a hard time of it. Then I was aware of a dark, almost black, hand reaching cautiously past my face in order to grasp Tom's hand. It was Plennik who wished to console Tom with a friendly gesture. But the black hand never got there. Ledin's virile, white face turned toward Plennik, and Plennik withdrew his hand. The tension between these two had been strong ever since the incident of the flare. Ledin no longer permitted Plennik to leave the hole. Over and over again Ledin's cold, grey eyes turned to Plennik and calmly lingered there. The scrutiny was clearly a torment to Plennik. Plennik had not suffered from thirst, fatigue, or cold. He knew that the moment was soon coming when he could rejoin his side. He knew that Tom and I would help him. And he knew also that Ledin read all of his thoughts, or at least suspected, and would be happy to do away with Plennik in military fashion. For that reason Tom and I, in turn, kept watch on Ledin. It was a painful game we played with each other, and the very silence and immobility in the hole created a tense, forbidding atmosphere that evening.

On one occasion Plennik's and Ledin's eyes chanced to meet, but neither of them turned away. Ledin must have taken this as a challenge, for his face, which was well shaven as usual, hardened and became handsomer. But Plennik was not even aware that he stared fixedly at Ledin. At that moment Plennik knew only one thing, that his ear had been assailed by a woman's song. And that woman was Lúnnaja.

The song, which seemed to come from very close by, was quite soft at the beginning. The rest of us were not aware of it. Moreover the wind blew directly at the singer and sometimes seized the very song from her lips. The voice was surrounded by noise and salvos of laughter. They were drinking and cheering themselves up in the enemy lines. Soldiers fell in with the melody, shouting and roaring. We were used to the like. But a moment later the female voice rose above its unworthy society and hung alone above the frozen trees, quivering with a warm, intense life, the life of a woman.

Without shaking off Ledin's glance, Plennik slowly stood up. As soon as Ledin became aware of the song, he got up also, but very quickly. At a moment like that Ledin might have been expected to lose control of his voice. But, on the contrary, it was good humored as he said:

"Well, well, so that's how it is. We can expect them here any minute. But we won't leave the spot until they are almost upon us. You know my orders. To your weapons!"

Every vestige of calm had left poor Plennik, perhaps all reason. It was both moving and comical to see how he tried to make himself invisible and to smuggle himself by Ledin in the direction of the ceiling exit. Ledin had something approaching a smile on his lips when he put his hand on Plennik's chest and let him have it. Plennik was thrown back to his place on the floor. But in a fraction of a second Plennik was back on his feet again and now he was violent. He was so unlike himself as to be almost unrecognizable, but his face was not contorted. Quite the contrary, it hung slack like that of a psychotic. His nostrils had flared out. His body seemed to contract and become shorter. Suddenly he sprang through the air directly at Ledin, threw him among the spruce boughs, and put a foot on his back as if to use it as a springboard toward the door. But Ledin was agile

76

and quick. He grabbed Plennik by one leg and struck him hard. What Plennik had intended was meaningless now, so Tom and I intervened in order to keep him there and calm him down. But the voice of Lúnnaja within him was stronger than anything else. He had the strength of ten men, and he swept us aside as easily as if he had suddenly acquired the paws of a bear. Suddenly I saw Ledin fingering something: a pistol. But just as quickly, I got, or pretended to get, the sharp blow of an elbow, a blow that threw me backwards and made me knock the carbide lamp from its hook in the ceiling. The light went out immediately. The darkness was impenetrable. Ledin could not shoot. Like a clenched fist the four of us lay in a heap among the spruce branches on the floor and held each other in a kind of cramped immobility. From where we lay we could hear that the wind had accelerated up there in the woods, nearing storm proportions. Sometimes, when it stopped for a moment as if to decide whom to assault next, the song reached us again. But then we heard what we had been waiting for: the attack.

It was nothing remarkable, nothing of epoch-making violence. Only a few hundred infantry weapons that simultaneously directed their fire over us. In all probability each of us was thinking one and the same thing as we lay there — that the flare had revealed a line of defense, not our miserable persons. The fortification, which consisted of some logs piled upon each other, had been used when we were still a company. Now the fortification lay quite empty, but this was not apparent from a distance. Several volleys of fire were directed at the fortification to see what happened. Nothing more remarkable than that. Immediately after the gunfire, they'd send a hundred or so men forward with bayonets fixed and pockets swelling with hand grenades. They would find the fortification empty, turn back, and report that we had withdrawn. It was not at all certain that they'd discover us in our holes. Possibly they'd celebrate a victory that very night, drinking vodka, turning up their radios, and hooting and shouting into the night. They were always in a good humor there on the other side. And if you got a "cheap victory," why try to pay more? It was a likable aspect to their character.

Nor were we who lay knotted together among the spruce boughs especially heroic either. I remember very well — and with some cause — that I lay there undermost in that heap of humanity and thought about death. The thought that visited me for the first time was that a man cannot die, not really, not at all. The most essential thing in us — that which lies at the heart of things, that which looks out from a man's eyes at the moment of death, that which is taken up by the one who loves us very much and whom we love — that thing is sorrow. It penetrates men's hearts for all time and becomes a part of them. From that moment onward we are a part of their actions, we live in their lives, and influence everything. It is "eternal life" and it is "the transformation of the soul." Thus love is the greatest force of all. It is everything.

CHAPTER 12

FOR YOUR SAKE,
COMRADES

The silence that follows an extended roar of gunfire is of a special kind. You can *hear* it. You enjoy the sound of it. It is as pleasurable, rich, and varied as the sound of a symphony. While it is playing, a soldier does not want to be disturbed. He wishes to be alone with himself, with the god within. The silence is like a choir of small, friendly birds that sit in every tree of the forest, and every bush, in the snow, on the frozen earth, and in the timbers of the trenches. The harmony exists in their vocal chords. They experience it ecstatically. But they do not give voice to it, because it isn't necessary. It simply exists.

Our little carbide lamp was burning once more. The walls were red from the light of the rectangular iron box, and there was the odor of roasted horsemeat. The Bouncer had arranged everything. And now the silence after the attack reigned over us all. The Bouncer had come fumbling at our cardboard door a moment after the silence ensued. We were still lying among the spruce boughs, Ledin, Tom, Plennik, and I. At first we thought it was the enemy who had found us in spite of the wind and intended to throw in some hand grenades. After all, there are on the other side some who are as brave and enterprising as the Bouncer, some who do not have time to listen to something that does not exist. But it was only the Bouncer, and even he was silent. He wanted to astound us with what he had accomplished, to present the result without any explanation, for the sake of the effect. We could figure things out for ourselves. It was plain that he had performed an act of heroism. You could tell it from his manner. It was also plain that he had stolen a sled which could be broken up for firewood. On the sled lay reindeer skins, some horsemeat, and black bread. He hung the bread up around the glowing stovepipe in order to thaw it out, then he moved about and took care of us in a fatherly fashion, as if he were a doctor among the desperately ill. His upper lip had swollen and stiffened even more and now lacked all feeling. In the warmth of the hole he was unaware that the drippings from his nose ran down over it. He tucked the reindeer skins in around us, without attending to himself. He passed the horsemeat politely, waiting until last to serve himself. He was unmistakably in his element. Finally, as soon as we had eaten and drunk, Ledin asked him if he had succeeded with the machine gun nest that looked like a face. To the surprise of everyone, the Bouncer answered:

"Machine gun nest? Face? No, I didn't do anything about that, Ledin." After a moment he added, "One thing at a time."

"I understand," said Ledin in a very friendly way "but . . ."

"It's absolutely necessary," insisted the Bouncer, with something of a higher officer's authority in his voice. "One thing at a time, that's always been my philosophy."

Ledin looked at him with an amused, somewhat ironic glint in his eyes.

"You did something else first?" asked Ledin.

The Bouncer sat down beside the stove, his legs crossed like an Oriental and the dogskin coat thrown loosely over his shoulders, creating a decorative impression, although the heat was, under the circumstances, beginning to be oppressive in the hole. He continued to eat enormously and his mouth was full of meat as he talked to Ledin.

"There was one thing," he explained, "one thing that I owed you boys, that I ought to do for your sakes."

He took the lump of meat from his mouth, gave Tom and me a friendly nod, laughed, and then tossed the lump back in again.

"For our sakes?" I asked.

"Exactly," he said. "If I said 'for your sakes,' I meant just that. For your sakes."

A silence fell over us, and the Bouncer took advantage of its strategic value; then he turned to Tom, pointed to his stiffened upper lip, and said:

"It doesn't bother me at all, Tom. I'm not mad at you because of it. Reward evil with good, that's what I say. But now to the point. It was a kind of revenge I took out in the snow on someone who did you harm. Or wished to do you harm."

"Oh?"

"Yes. And since I think there is such a thing as honor among comrades, and I think so highly of all of you . . ."

"So what happened?" said Tom.

"So I took revenge. It's as simple as that."

"But on what?" I asked in irritation.

The Bouncer opened a little door in the stove, blew his nose carefully into his hand, threw the results into the fire, and watched with curious eyes how the snot began to jump agitatedly back and forth on a burning piece of wood, emitting a popping sound and finally exploding. Then he laid his head back, opened his mouth wide, and laughed. Suddenly he became very serious and said in an almost troubled tone of voice:

"Well, you see, perhaps it's not such a pretty story, but you see . . . there was . . . a woman."

I threw a quick look at Tom. He was staring fixedly at his brother with black foreboding painted over his dirt-covered face.

"A woman?" said Ledin, interested.

The Bouncer looked up and a smile broke all over his face.

"A woman," he answered.

"Whatever you may think," he continued, "there are women out here in the snow too. At least one or two. Not on our side, but over there."

With his index finger crooked he fished a couple of meat chunks out of the pot and looked them over carefully as if he were choosing between them. He seemed to sense that the silence from the direction of Tom and me was in some way charged, and so he turned to us and blurted out:

81

"What do you know! I think these fine gentlemen are pricking up their ears a little! Well, you can't be blamed for that. After all, it has been quite a while since you saw a woman last, hasn't it? Or had one? Right? And felt the softness of her, as you might say. Hasn't it?"

Once more he threw his head back, his neck swelled, and he sent a salvo of laughter up toward the ceiling.

"Well," he said, his voice full of understanding, "sex has its importance, sex too. It isn't easy to live month after month without knowing the feel of a woman's soft flesh . . ."

"You've known it, then?" asked Ledin.

"Maybe, my dear Ledin," answered the Bouncer.

"Tonight? This night?"

The Bouncer nodded mysteriously.

"In the woods?" Ledin asked.

"It isn't so unlikely is it? Unless a man's a homebody by nature, he's got to experience a little of everything. Even out here."

Suddenly he kissed his chunk of meat, kissed it three or four times, laughed with delight, and continued:

"A charming woman! God in heaven, what a charming woman!"

And then he changed his tone, began to speak soberly and matter-of-factly, raising his eyebrows and gazing at us:

"You haven't already forgotten how the night's attack began, have you? I can't believe it. Don't you think it was carefully planned? A woman singing out there so as to make a man's guts turn inside out! Especially a man on guard duty. Soldiers on guard duty aren't any less men for that. And what a song! What a song!"

The Bouncer carefully put his chunk of meat on Plennik's knee, as if Plennik were an inanimate object, got up, and stood with his back against the red-brown of the earth wall. Then he shut his eyes and began to sing.

The Bouncer was musical. He had a clear, somewhat high tenor that was quite pleasant to hear. And it surprised us all how expertly he improvised, imitating the song that we had heard from the other side. He sang without moving his lips, and his expression was solemn, almost touching, like that of a sleeping child.

Plennik sat just behind me, and I could not see him at all; nevertheless I had an uncomfortably intense awareness of his whole being. I had a feeling that his small eyes, the color of a spring sky, were wide open and drinking in everything around him with a terrifying sensitivity. Tom sat quite motionless looking down into the spruce branches, without thinking to finger the fat ridges on his forehead. He looked like a man condemned to death.

I seized the Bouncer by the dogskin coat which was still hanging over his shoulders and tried to stop him.

"The song doesn't interest us in the least," I explained.

But Ledin, who was a "fair" superior officer and readily permitted a soldier some leeway if it was within reason, broke in immediately.

"Mind your own business," he said calmly, but with a glance that told me he really meant it.

Tom and I sat there powerless. We had kept from both Ledin and the Bouncer everything we knew about Plennik and Lúnnaja, everything that was told me on that night in Kámenka, and everything that I had heard the same night from the other side of the mine field. Explanations and revelations at a time like this would be enough to put Ledin quite out of his mind. He would, and perhaps justifiably, be filled with a consuming fury under a calm, controlled exterior. He might give just any kind of order, not only to me, but also to Plennik and Tom. I had an overwhelming feeling of responsibility; my conscience was confused and tormented. But the Bouncer continued till the end of the song.

When he had finished, he looked at us cautiously as if he expected a little praise and he did not hide his astonishment at our pained expressions.

"Boys, what's the matter with you?" he asked, clearly disappointed. "Aren't you feeling good?"

He could find no other explanation than that we had eaten too much horsemeat, and so he began to joke immediately. If we couldn't smile or laugh any longer, he said, then we ought to neigh. Nobody would be annoyed. Nothing could destroy his good humor that evening.

He sat back down again, took the chunk of meat from Plennik's knee, brushed it off, and continued to eat.

"It was beautiful," he mumbled. "You can't deny it. It was one hell of a beautiful song. And, I'll tell you, boys, the woman who sang it — she was the one I met."

He emitted a loud belch that sounded like some kind of internal avalanche, smiled, excused himself, belched again, and continued, clearly having experienced some relief:

"I came upon her during the height of the gunfire. It's a good thing that you did not return it, boys. A very good thing. You are a sharp leader, you are, Ledin. You ought to be an officer, mark my word. Naturally they got the impression that we had abandoned the woods since the fortification lay empty and the trenches around about were also apparently vacated. Now they'll calm down at least until the wind stops. They pulled back immediately. I knew that for sure. But the sled — I stole that. I would have been a fool not to. And there was another thing I stole, too, I must admit."

He laughed until he was quite red in the face, laughed until he was interrupted by a violent attack of coughing. Then his voice sank to a whisper:

"She was beautiful. Beautiful as a queen. A beauty, a beauty, a real beauty . . ."

"Well," he continued, in a rather more calculating manner, "I've had a fair amount of experience with beautiful women in my life, I won't deny it, but one built like this one — ! Just to touch her . . . God in heaven! Just the feel of her breath . . . God in heaven!"

Suddenly the Bouncer noticed Plennik, who had been almost imperceptibly drawing closer to him. It was as if Plennik had caught some scent, animal-like, with all his animal senses, and his face looked as if it were illuminated from within by an intense blue-white carbide flame. He had caught the drift of everything. The Bouncer slapped him hard on the shoulder.

"Old man," he chortled, "what a woman to get your hands on!"

Suddenly he became serious and looked with a frown, first at Tom and then at me.

"I really don't understand what's eating you fellows," he said reproachfully. "You look as nervous as a confirmation class. Haven't I got a right to talk? You're just jealous, that's all."

"We're tired, Bouncer," I said, and turned to Ledin. "Can't you make him be quiet so we can get some sleep?"

But Ledin paid no attention to me. He lit a cigarette, offered the Bouncer one, and gave him a sign to continue.

"You understand," resumed the Bouncer, encouraged, "that this thing of beauty had been with the soldiers for some time before the attack. It's smart to have dames along. Makes soldiers want to distinguish themselves and do their best. So it's smart.

"But," he continued, taking a deep drag on his cigarette, "you understand that she wasn't right there in the lines. She was a little to the side, out of the range of fire. And right on the path to that machine gun nest I was going to take and *will* take. As sure as I am the Bouncer."

He sat thinking for a few minutes and then continued:

"The remarkable thing was that it was she who pounced on me and not the other way around. Sure, other women have run after the Bouncer before, but not in just that way. Not straight as an arrow. I heard her come running through the deep snow, and I dived out of sight under a spruce tree. How did I know it was a woman? She stopped just a little way from me, on that sled, and began to sing. When she had finished, she crept under the sled and lay there while the shooting was going on, sixty, perhaps seventy, meters away. She lay there until the gunfire had stopped, and then she turned back. It was then that she passed the tree where I was lying. First she went on by; then she stopped a moment, and began to walk around the tree. She must have smelled the fur coat. I can't explain it any other way. Then she said something. I don't know what. When I didn't answer, she cautiously bent back a couple of branches and came nearer. Then I grabbed her like a flash of lightning, and pulled her to me. I had thought immediately, no, I won't shoot her. Absolutely not. If I do, I'll have the whole company on my neck. And I know what they'd be likely to do under such circumstances. But I won't let her go either, for then she would report that someone was snooping around in the neighborhood of that machine gun nest that looks like a face. And I'm going to take that machine gun nest, sooner or later, of that I'm sure. Then I thought like this: shouldn't I hold her tight and *stab* her instead with a bayonet? What do you say? What? Wasn't I right? In a situation like that?"

The Bouncer stood up. He hauled out his bayonet and thrust it into the air a few times. Then Tom spoke with a great effort:

"Put the bayonet away."

"Don't you understand what you are doing to Plennik," I said. "It's his people you're talking about."

86

"You gentlemen are so sensitive tonight," Ledin said with great sarcasm. "What's the meaning of it?"

"Ledin," I said. "Listen to me. Plennik is sick. Look at him. Look at his eyes. If I take him out for a little . . ."

Ledin bent down and looked at Plennik. With the help of signs and gestures, he asked him if he wanted to go out. But naturally Plennik did not want to. He wanted to learn more. His mouth was hot and dry. There was nothing that Tom and I could do.

"Now you are going to hear something," the Bouncer continued, his voice raised. "The tree I had hidden myself under was a little larger than the others. It was like a little cave under the lowest branches, and there wasn't much snow down there. It was warmer too. I lay there and pulled the woman to me; it was her own fault. She could have gone on by and not started nosing around there. Then I wouldn't have had to . . ."

Silence reigned for a time. The Bouncer had sat back down again and assumed a sulky expression. Then Ledin spoke in a low, serious voice:

"Did you stab her?"

The Bouncer roused himself and looked about.

"No!" and then he exclaimed: "My how impatient and curious you are all of a sudden! You, too, Ledin! And you others are fairly white in the face. Who would have thought it!"

He laid back his head, raised the stiffened upper lip, and uttered a short, hard laugh.

"I must say," he continued, "I like it that you want to hear my story. Before, you just wanted to pick on me and run me down, and nobody cared anything about me. But now all that's changed. I guess at bottom we were always good comrades though. It just didn't come to the surface."

"So you didn't stab her?" I said.

"Hold on," he said and stood up. "You'll see in good time.

We tumbled about and struggled a while in the hole. She sensed that I was not one of her people, it was clear. I would never have believed that a woman could be so strong. It didn't seem possible. To keep her from screaming and attracting help, I clamped my hand over her mouth. She bit me, but I had gloves on. And to touch her — that was a strange feeling. It was funny that in spite of having my coat on, I could still feel the suppleness of her body and then . . ."

"So you didn't do anything to her?" I broke in impatiently. "You didn't want to?"

"Want to? Of course a man doesn't want to. It's no pleasure. But you can't be too soft, either, out here. Can you?"

He looked feverishly about.

"You know what I did?" he said.

"No."

"I wouldn't have bothered to tell you before, when you were always and forever taunting me. But now that we are better comrades, as it were . . . Well, you see, I . . . I *kissed* her."

He looked around somewhat uncertainly, but when no one laughed, he continued with more assurance:

"I kissed her as she had never been kissed before in her whole life. It wasn't the first time I ever kissed a beautiful woman. You can depend on that."

"And then you left her?" I asked impatiently. "You separated?"

"Of course we separated," he answered. "I don't have her with me, do I? You see, I thought like this: if I take her prisoner, she'd be good to have around. But then I thought, no, it isn't worth it. Considering how you mocked me and picked on me when I brought back that Plettnik, or whatever he's called, it isn't worth it. And what would you think if I came back trailing a dame behind me!"

He laughed with some embarrassment.

"But you aren't that way now," he said finally, and his face was full of honest, good-humored gratitude. "You've grown out of it. And it's kind of strange. It was as if already out there in the snow I had a feeling that we had become better friends, even before it really happened. When I was holding that woman under me and thinking that it was she who sang and maybe caused your death, both yours" — the Bouncer gave me a friendly look — "and yours, Ledin, and yours, Tom, then I felt a desire for vengeance, stronger than anything I've felt in my whole life, and then the point of the bayonet crept close to her breast as if under its own power. First it struck something hard, a piece of bread that she was carrying close to her heart. But then the bread fell to the side and then . . ."

He pulled the blade of the bayonet out of its sheath.

"Then I *stuck* . . ."

The blade was coated with a thin, yellow-red film of blood. Plennik stood up, looking at it all the time.

An intolerable silence followed. Terrified, the Bouncer took a step backward and looked in helpless confusion from one of us to the other.

His swollen upper lip was twisted.

CHAPTER 13

THE
SECRET THOUGHT
OF DYING

I say to the Bouncer's and Tom's little mother:

"So passed a woman's soul, a dream, and a longing, into 'eternal life'!"

We are no more remarkable than is the grass of the earth.

89

Why? The grass grows low and is suffocated by the shadows of the forest. It yearns for light, air, and the warmth of the sun. After millennia of longing, hereditary longing, small gripping tendrils develop on the stalks. The low grass has become a clinging growth that can climb up tree trunks toward the light, the air, and the sun.

Is it any more remarkable that within us we bear all the longings of the dead, all the possibilities of the unborn?

Man longs eternally after the most momentous of all powers — that of love. It is a force which, if we possessed it uncorrupted or almost uncorrupted, would give us the strength and authority of a Jesus Christ or St. Francis of Assisi.

To be able to love is to believe.

Tom wanted to get drunk. He often used to drink out there when something filled him full of spiritual disgust. He could drink himself quite helpless, and he would maintain that intoxication was a "partial suicide." He knew also that he was the kind of man who all his life wages war upon himself in order to "arrive at a conclusion." In contrast to his brother, he did not believe himself capable of anything at all. He knew from the moment that he began something that it was sure to fail, and for that reason he engaged himself as little as possible, said as little as possible, in order to "do the least harm." His most natural pose was to lie stretched out on a skin rug with his hands under his head and an expression on his face that reflected all the troubles of the world, even when he slept — or perhaps especially then. We used to stand watching Tom when he slept, and we were astonished at the dumb cry of pain that spread over his ugly face. The Bouncer would laugh in embarrassment.

When Tom drank a good deal, he always reached a certain stage where he began to dance. In some ways the

dance was heart-rending to see. It betrayed and under-
lined that which was beyond redemption in his nature. His
dance was an expression of contempt for himself, for his
clumsiness and his joylessness. His thick lips would assume
a bitter grimace. He lifted his feet alternately, raised and
lowered his shoulders, and cut the air with his great, flat
hands. That was all. But he would continue for some time
with this macabre exhibition, a critical self-observer's flag-
ellation of his own image.

A day and a half after the Bouncer demonstrated his
cordiality toward us all with the account of his vengeance
on the foreign woman, we found ourselves, Tom and I,
out in the snow at just that place where the enemy attack
had originated. We searched for Lúnnaja for a little while,
but that was not our real mission. We knew anyway that
the Bouncer had made off with her immediately after his
revenge and hidden her somewhere beneath the snow. And
the wind had wiped out all tracks. No, our mission was to
look for vodka bottles, not fully emptied, and the fact is
that we came upon a good many. It was that hour of the
day when the air hangs heavy and sticky, like grey spider-
webs, not yet really dry. Tom poured all the remains into
a couple of larger bottles and then said to me with a little
smile:

"There, brother. Now I have about enough for one dance
demonstration . . ."

We started back. When we reached a point about halfway between our old fortifications, now covered with new
snow, and the occupied earth-pits deep within the woods,
Tom, who walked ahead, turned to me and said in a low
voice:

"Look!"

It was Ledin whom he had detected among the trees.
Ledin's physique permitted him to move upon the snowed-

91

over paths with a certain grace and ease, but we neverthe-less decided that his unusual equilibrium meant something special just now.

We were certain of one thing. Since yesterday Ledin had had it in for us, Tom and me. He had sat and observed our reactions while the Bouncer recounted his experience with Lúnnaja. He clearly thought that we were keeping something hidden from him. All day yesterday we had had a feeling that Ledin was giving us a certain period of res-pite while he waited for the confession of what we kept in secrecy. He would never stoop to solicit a confession. But he had hung around in our company more than usual, staged artful silences, and created favorable situations to drop some pointed remark or other. But Tom and I kept our silence. And each time that Ledin's eyes moved in our di-rection, they became clearer and younger, a change that meant he hated us.

Finally when he came toward us, we knew that he had reached a decision. Nevertheless I made a clumsy effort. I gave him a friendly smile, nodded, and stepped to the side. He came very close to us, stood between us, and laid one hand on Tom's shoulder, the other hand on mine. We had never before seen his face at such close quarters and by daylight, although a very poor excuse for daylight. Real-ly we saw only the chin area quite clearly. He was, as al-ways, unusually clean-shaven, but the rest of his face, which had not had any contact with shaving soap, was grey with dirt and merged, as it were, into the spiderweb-grey light all around. We could see his mouth clearly, and a little smile played around it. It began to speak calmly, ami-ably, and with restraint. It began by saying that a certain affair was very sad indeed — namely, Plennik's condition. For more than a day Plennik had sat hunched up, com-pletely apathetic, with his empty eyes shut most of the time.

92

He ate nothing, drank nothing, smoked not at all, said nothing. It was a shame about the man, Ledin said, an enormous shame about him. It was enough to tear your heart just to look at him.

Ledin paused for some time, looked at Tom, looked at me, and let his hands play on our shoulders as if he were petting us. When he spoke again, his speech was interrupted by long intervals. He said he didn't know . . . the real . . . cause . . . that he could see . . . that Plennik was in distress . . . and that Plennik ought to be freed . . . from his distress.

Ledin stressed the firmness of his decision by immediately leaving us, after making a playful gesture in the direction of my automatic pistol and saying:

"You two are to take care of the matter. With this. And you ought to be finished within, let us say, five hours."

We watched him continue his walk down toward the fortifications.

When we got back, we found Plennik sitting alone in the hole precisely as Ledin had described. We caught no more than a glimpse of the Bouncer in between two of the holes where he was trying to persuade someone to accompany him on his foray against the machine gun nest. But he seemed to be getting a poor reception everywhere.

Tom fired the stove. We had recently got permission to fetch wood from more distant places. Then Tom set about warming the vodka. It had been lying out in the snow, which was nearly 20 degrees below. Tom, the unlucky bird, had on an earlier occasion drunk vodka without this precaution and burned his intestines with the fluid cold. We sat there in silence.

Once when I looked at Plennik his eyes were open, almost staring. They were directed at the vodka bottles. So I spoke:

"Do you want some? It's vodka."

He hesitated some time before he answered.

"I want some," he said. "All of it."

I looked at him in astonishment.

"Yes," he said. "And when I've drunk it, then I'd like to take a little walk."

I understood him immediately. He wanted to get himself thoroughly drunk, walk out into the snow, lie down, and sleep a deep sleep. A very pleasant way to die. I explained how it was to Tom. He nodded.

"It's the best way. You and I could not bring ourselves to put a shot into him," he said.

I saw that Tom's hands were shaking and that his face twitched. It was difficult for him to refrain from drinking since his throat was conditioned to alcohol. But he did not take a drop.

Plennik drank. He drank as if the liquor were milk. By the time he had emptied the first bottle, we still could see no noticeable change in him. But as he began a new bottle, we noticed that one eyelid drooped lower than the other and could not be raised again. Then his face began to assume the expressions of one who is listening to conversation or who is himself talking. He was clearly addressing himself. And in a few minutes he began to talk aloud, but very thickly, thoroughly exhausted. I could not understand all he said, but one word kept repeating itself: hunchbacks. It sometimes seemed that he looked at Tom and me when he spoke that word, and since it didn't seem in his nature to insult anyone, I thought his anguish had befuddled him. Among other things, he said that we who were in the hole were volunteers in the war and that therefore we *were* the war. He repeated the assertion over and over again, sometimes taking long pauses as if he had dozed off, but coming to again and drinking from the vodka. He said he

94

could understand us, because he himself was once a hunch-back. He had stood with a stone raised high over another man, Father Timofej. Actually he had wished to destroy himself then. We had wished the same thing, he said, when we signed up in the war.

He directed his gaze downward at the spruce branches and mumbled gloomily that men *seek* something at the front — otherwise they wouldn't be there. Suddenly he raised his head and said in a loud, clear voice:

"In the face of death, so much that is twisted in us is straightened out. Our hunched backs are straightened out. They are hammered out with blows. With blows!"

He put the bottle to his mouth and took a sturdy pull at it. I had difficulty understanding him, but he said something to the effect that at the front there is a little fragment of heaven that attracts you by its purity — and that was what was so terrible. That's why there will always be war. "It's funny," he said, "that you can take a map, an ordinary printed map, bought in a store, draw a thin line on the map, and say: "Heaven and hell meet at just this line. That's the front. No matter how thin you draw the line, it will be too thick. You can't draw it fine enough with a pen; the line is so precise and sharply defined. It is a strange thing," he said.

And for a long time he sat sunk in thought about the line that was so uncommonly thin. Then he roused himself, took a drink, and said in a loud voice:

"No man in human history has gone to the front with the secret thought of killing. He has gone with the secret thought of dying."

He changed his position, this time kneeling, and continued in a whisper:

"When a man is eye to eye with the enemy or lying curled up in the cold of night by a dying reindeer who will soon be as cold and hard as its own antlers, then . . . then something remarkable happens."

Tom and I were looking at him, but I don't believe he even noticed us. He was talking to himself as if he were alone.

"Oh yes," he repeated, "something remarkable happens. It is that holy moment when nothing visible happens and yet the greatest thing of all.

"The holy hour," he continued "unstained by words or thoughts. The hour when a man's head becomes as motionless and silent as a reindeer's head under its crown of horns. — That slow moment when he is born into the animal's dignity. Into himself."

He stood up to full height, but then his legs betrayed him and he sank back down again. He smiled gravely and said with deliberation:

"The collapse, I tell you, sometimes destroys just that distant thing which is the cause of the collapse, and wipes it out! To hell with it! Or to hell with us!"

He raised the bottle to his lips and emptied it. The sagging eyelid had sunk even lower.

"They're playing!" he said, looking up suddenly. "They're playing, the black ones! They're playing for us! They like to play for hunchbacks. Do you hear them scattered out there in the snow reaching for their instruments? Do you hear them! They're playing merry songs . . ."

He listened for a long time. Then he stood up, this time without falling. He opened the ceiling door, listened, and clambered out into the cold.

Tom and I followed him.

No northern lights illuminated the sky. Everything was silent and black. We could hear his steps in front of us and occasionally glimpse his heels. He went down to the fortifications, crossed the clearing, and continued into the woods. Once there, Tom and I stopped and waited till we no longer heard his steps in the snow. Then I raised my automatic pistol and fired — for Ledin's benefit — a short volley straight up into the treetops.

Then we turned and went back at a brisk pace.

CHAPTER 14

THE CAP
THAT FLEW UP
IN THE AIR

The appearance of the aurora borealis was both striking and sudden that evening. It wasn't so much like light playing against a dark sky as it was the dark playing against the light. It was as if a giant searchlight were directed straight up at the sky, and as if dancing, gesticulating bodies of men on the lens projected a wild dance onto the zenith.

Tom and I lay alone in the hole, trying to sleep, while the Bouncer was out on his mission. We had just returned after following Plennik "to his rest" out in the snow, and the thought of him did not relax its grip on our hearts. When Ledin jumped back into the hole, I lied right in his face.

"Yes," I said, "now it's done, Ledin."

"Is that so?" he said.

"Maybe it was best that way," I continued, embroidering. "Plennik was suffering. I admit it."

Both Tom and I lay with our eyes shut, but we sensed that Ledin stood there searching our faces, which were intensely lighted by the carbide lamp at the ceiling. I had to talk a good deal to keep my face from betraying me.

"I put the shots in the back of his neck," I said, "all of them. Did you hear?"

"Yes."

"Tom wanted to stop me."

"So?"

"Yes, he wanted to stop me. And I understand him. In fact, I didn't think I could go through with it myself. But I did."

Ledin merely stood there watching us.

"It was odd," I lied, "that his cap flew off when I fired the shots. It must have been the vapor from the barrel that did it. I held the muzzle tight against his neck."

"So?"

"Yes, his cap flew straight up into the air, almost a meter. It looked crazy."

I said no more, nor did Ledin. A long silence followed. Sometimes it was as if Ledin no longer stood there, but I knew he did. I knew that he continued to search my face and waited to catch my gaze. The temptation to open my eyes was almost agonizing. But I held out. I did not look up. I did not betray myself by so much as a quiver of an eyelid. I beat him at the game. Tom and I both understood this only moments later, when a strong odor of coffee began to permeate the hole. Ledin had a little coffee left, and, while he did not drink coffee himself, he offered it to his men from time to time. When they did something to earn it. While we drank, Ledin talked. He was an intelligent man, and when he wished he could give the impression of being very amiable. He talked about trivialities, about socks that got frozen in boots and had to be pried loose with a bayonet, about nails that stopped growing in the cold, but he also told us that the Bouncer had the second time gone out after the machine gun nest in the woods, the one that "looked like a face." It ought to be there still, the Bouncer had assured him, in spite of the fact that all signs of the enemy had completely disappeared everywhere about us. Ledin treated himself to a small, compassionate smile when he spoke of "the good Bouncer."

At that moment the Bouncer was somewhere out in the forest under a sky more and more agitated by the northern lights. Tom and I had scarcely caught a glimpse of him since the adventure with the woman in the woods. But his perplexity that he might have done something irrational, although he couldn't quite understand how, had already left him, and his self-assurance had returned. Still ahead of him was the failure of his second heroic one-man expedition against the machine gun nest. He later opened his heart to me and told me just what happened.

The wind was strong as he passed the fortifications on the way into the forest. It was of a special kind, not ripping up the snow in great swirls, but floating like an ice-cold stream from the north — fast, hard, and soundless — over the surface of the snow. The Bouncer had to proceed against the current of cold and it was hard work. As he reached the middle of the clearing just beyond the fortifications, he suddenly stopped and crouched down. He had heard something that astounded him — the distant sound of church bells coming to him out of the darkness.

A hot wave of blood suffused the nape of his neck. He knew that the nearest church bells were a hundred or more kilometers away, and where they existed — if they existed — they had not been used for years. He had a half instinctive feeling that somebody was playing a joke on him. His swollen upper lip twisted into a sheepish smile and he heard himself hiss:

"Crazy. Church bells? Crazy."

He quickened his pace, but the church bells continued to hound him. He pressed the flaps of his fur cap closer to his ears and pulled the hood of the *anorak* all the way over his head. But he heard them anyway — not always, but from time to time. He began to run in order to stir up his circulation, but the bells followed him even more pitilessly as he ran. He decided on quite a different course of action, a more manly one: to look the danger right in the eye. He stopped, stood quite still, threw back the hood of the *anorak*, and removed his cap. In spite of the cold, he bared his ears and listened intently. But then the bells stopped. He had noticed earlier that when he stopped the sound disappeared. No matter how hard he listened, he could hear nothing — no sound of distant bells. But he thought he heard something else, something almost as implausible as church bells. He stood as if paralyzed in the snow and did not wish to believe his ears. What sounded like a human lament, or some kind of groaning, came from a location near him. He was a courageous man and decided to meet the danger head on.

The snow itself created a pale, pale light. Trees could be distinguished and among them certain oblong objects, blackly silhouetted against the snow. It was the "dark ones," the dead, hard as stone. He had passed hundreds of them on his mission and they had not bothered him. He had merely clambered over them, but now he had taken no more than a step when he halted. His vision swam. Right at his feet lay one of the "dark ones" — moving a little. An outstretched arm had moved, almost imperceptibly, but moved nevertheless.

The Bouncer stood still, waiting. But now he neither saw nor heard anything. Then he decided to prod the outstretched arm of the body with his foot. And the arm moved . . .

It was alive. At the very moment the Bouncer brought his gun down from his shoulder, a strong odor of alcohol assailed his nostrils. He bent down, pulled out a pocket flashlight, and shone it on the prostrate figure. It was Plennik.

The Bouncer was astonished to find Plennik out there and in such a drunken condition, and it was some moments before he did anything. He knew nothing of Ledin's order. He pulled out a scrap of wool cloth, massaged Plennik's face, which in spots was as white as marble, and then wrapped him up in the dogskin coat, threw him over his shoulder, and began the journey back. But after a few meters he stopped and put his burden down again in the snow.

Doubt had suddenly assailed him as to what to do. It occurred to him that Ledin had always wanted to be rid of Plennik, but he also thought of his brother Tom — Tom, who had been so troubled and melancholy these past days. He knew that Tom would be happy that Plennik had been saved from death by exposure. — But Ledin would be angry. — Well, in any case, Tom would be grateful. — Still, Ledin was commander out here. — On the other hand, Tom was his own brother.

The Bouncer threw Plennik over his shoulder, carried him some distance further, turned around, put him down in the snow, picked him up again, continued for a time, and then his doubts began all over again. He had begun to talk aloud to himself, and he was thoroughly miserable at heart. Another thing perplexed and frightened him: every time he reversed direction to return Plennik to his resting place in the snow, he heard again the distant clamor-

101

ing sound of bells. But when he carried Plennik in the direction of the trenches, the sound stopped. So he stopped worrying over the matter and carried Plennik homeward toward the trenches.

It took all his strength. Sometimes he collapsed heavily into the drifts with his burden, but then he stood up and struggled stubbornly onward through the snow. His underclothes became soaked with sweat, but he didn't give up. He saw his brother's face in front of him — and it wore an expression of admiration for the Bouncer. He heard Tom's voice speaking in a grateful, friendly tone — directly to the Bouncer . . .

But suddenly he stopped, stood quite motionless for a moment, and then began to laugh. A thought had occurred to him though he hardly knew how. It had to do with the church bells. It became unexpectedly clear to him that the sound of the distant bells originated from the double barrel of his gun. He heard the sound as long as he moved against the wind, but when he was with the wind, it was silent. The Bouncer put Plennik down and experimented with this phenomenon. He was right, and he smiled broadly. But during the brief moment he stood still, his sweat-drenched underclothes froze stiff, forming knife-sharp edges at every fold. As he proceeded with his burden, the edges sawed into his flesh, chafed his testicles and knee-joints skinless, and made the fresh sweat burn like fire. But the Bouncer thought about his brother's face and how it would light up with happiness at Plennik's rescue, and he forced himself onward, homeward. By the time he was within sight of the four arm-thick pillars of fire over the earth-pockets, he was contorted into a caricature of himself.

Meanwhile Tom and I lay in the hole having a reason-

102

ably pleasant time while we listened to Ledin chatter ami- ably and tell stories interspersed with bursts of laughter. He exerted all his charms on us and plied us with cigarettes and coffee. He showed us snapshots of his fiancée and bolstered us with tributes to our reliability as soldiers.

Just then the roof door opened. The Bouncer crawled in puffing violently. His entire figure was covered with a thick layer of ice, and his face was white with a frost that ad- hered to every invisible hair. Heavy icicles hung from his swollen upper lip down to his chin. We were surprised that he was not wearing the dogskin coat, but just then he hauled it in and dumped it among the spruce branches on the floor. Then he began to prod it open with his foot, speaking not a word but keeping an eye on his brother Tom. His face cracked into a stiff smile.

In the coat lay Plennik. He lay on his side, the nape of his neck toward Ledin. There was no sign of a bullet hole there.

Ledin had sprung to his feet. Neither Tom nor I looked at him. Instead we looked at Plennik, who was clearly in bad shape. His breathing was faint and his eyelids were half closed over eyes that saw nothing. Tom and I remained completely motionless. It was so silent down there in the little hole that we could hear the ice crack on the Bouncer's face as a look of perplexity broke over it.

We had no idea how much time passed before Ledin said in a low deliberate voice, hardly above a whisper:

"Tomorrow, just before dawn, get out. Both of you. Try to find a way. Through the mine fields."

He meant Tom and me.

Then we heard Ledin leap out through the roof door, as agile as usual or perhaps more so. The Bouncer remained. He had slowly sunk back on his heels into his niche in the earthen wall.

103

CHAPTER 15

THE FACE
OF A TRANQUIL
CHILD

We are both very tired, the old lady and I, sitting there at the table. When people are tired, they learn a great deal about each other, perhaps because they haven't the strength to lie inwardly. The spring night is thin and cold, dawn is on the way, and I can just distinguish an object at a distance in the room, looking for all the world like a giant cockroach creeping up the wall. It is an old-fashioned telephone. We have a feeling that we ourselves consist of that almost nonexistent light that surrounds us. It is a light resembling a doubt. A neurosis, a life-doubt. That life-doubt which is one and the same even when it assumes exactly contrary expressions as it did with Tom and his brother: the one incapable of living, of acting and "being," the other in flight from himself in his panting fever to "be." It is a doubt from which we want to wrench ourselves — violently, desperately fighting — like crawfish in the mud when they try to cast off their tight, suffocating shells. Sometimes there are disasters in the river bottom, when the shells win the struggle. The creatures die from exhaustion. — But I continue my account for the old lady.

Tom and I were on our way to the mine fields as Ledin had commanded. He followed us for a stretch; he was a man with a sense of propriety. We left on skis without farewells, without even saying goodbye to Plennik, who lay dull and apathetic in his hole, or to the Bouncer who had disappeared without a trace around midnight. Now it was morning, with the grey light preparing itself to creep up over the horizon. It was dead calm.

The woods looked different today. During the recent heavy wind hundreds of bullet-riddled trees had collapsed, and now we had to work our way forward in zigzag fashion, fighting through a chaos of timber and underbrush. When we saw Ledin make a sign to stop, the faint hope crossed our minds that he would retract his order and torment us no more. Suddenly he threw himself to the ground. Tom and I did likewise. Close to a tree which still remained standing, in the vicinity of the sulfurously shining urine grotto, sat a new figure — at least we thought it was a figure, a man, someone we had never seen before. Ledin shouted something to him, but got no answer. We lay quiet several minutes, trying to see, but then crept closer. I called out in Russian, but got no answer either. In any case we could now see that it was a man, a soldier. He sat quite still holding something in his arms, something we couldn't get any impression of at all. Since he directed no weapon at us, Ledin arose from the snow and walked toward him. Tom and I followed.

The motionless one was our old friend the Bouncer. He sat holding something in his hands, a curious grey object. His head was thrown back and his face turned upwards. His skin was as hard and white as marble. His position indicated that he had sat fingering that object in his embrace until he fell asleep. And froze to death.

When we investigated the grey object, we understood why he had not hurried back over the little stretch he had left. The object was a decoy. A construction of pasteboard fashioned like a large automatic weapon. It looked like a face with eyes, wide mouth, and barrel for a nose. A great, surprised face.

Suddenly we understood everything. Expertly, perhaps

in exemplary fashion, the Bouncer had stolen around the nest and attacked from behind. Heroically. Alone. He had come rushing out of the darkness with tremendous power, snow spraying around his dogskin coat and his bayonet lowered. He had captured that fragment of cardboard so artfully erected like a kind of scarecrow.

We also understood why the Bouncer had thrown himself down in the snow to rest. Or to think. He had sat wondering whether he was a hero now — in spite of everything. Or just ludicrous. Or a ludicrous hero.

So he must have sat, irresolutely, at the base of the tree. He could already hear the thunderous laughter of contempt that would greet his homecoming to the trenches after the conquest of this "nest" he had talked about for so long.

So he must have sat and thought. Humble. Humiliated. And so he fell asleep.

He sat with his feet pulled in under him, and it appeared that, in death, he had gathered in his great limbs so as not to get in anybody's way.

The pale grey light fell upon his face. It was the face of a tranquil child, and the swollen upper lip was thrust forward like a newly born baby's.

CHAPTER 16

BREAKING CAMP

It was only a few minutes after the discovery of the Bouncer that Tom and I, advancing toward the mine fields, reached the little clearing in the woods where there was clean snow

— as if women had spread white sheets on the ground, the place we loved for its infinite purity. The place where the "signals," resembling telephone signals, surprised us, struck Tom down, and made my otherwise silent friend prattle and mutter so much while he crept about.

I know it's childish of me, but I was glad it was at just that spot in the woods, the most beautiful we knew, that Tom should remain lying. And it was bound to happen. From the moment Ledin gave the order to cross the mine fields, Tom had gone around with a suggestion of shamed confusion on his dark, negroid face, where the bright red "whiplash" from his cap shone the more intensely. Indeed the skin itself seemed to darken when he was about to undertake something that was sure to fail. He knew very well what would happen. And I could not help him.

When Tom was dead and I stood there alone in the white snow, I heard once more the sound of swallows crying in the sky. It was the creak of ski poles, the same sound as when the invisible one disappeared, the one who surprised Tom with the "signals." The sound was now coming directly toward me. I dug down into the snow and raised my automatic pistol.

But it was Ledin. He came gliding toward us with tremendous speed and strength, as elegantly as if he were putting on an exhibition. He was enjoying himself. He always did. He had heard the "signals." He understood everything that had happened, without asking a question, just by looking at me. He didn't address his attention to Tom for a moment. His sweaty intensity frightened me. He was somehow incandescent. A single thought consumed him: the moment was at hand for all of us to leave this wood forever.

We were to break camp immediately, all twenty of us — no, eighteen. We would follow the tracks of the man who shot Tom. The tracks were clear. There was a little light in the air and no breeze. He who shot Tom must have got himself through the treacherous areas by means of a mine chart. All we had to do was follow him. A new life lay beyond the mine fields, perhaps a better one, and in any case a different one. I tried to keep up with Ledin's violent pace on the way back to the holes to order decampment.

Once again I stood before the little, frozen sheet of cardboard that covered the entrance to our old home which now, for the first time, struck me as oppressive and uninviting. I could feel Ledin's eyes following me, but I had nothing special to do there. Then from down below I heard something that I had not expected to hear. It was Plennik speaking to someone. In his mother tongue.

I jumped down to him and saw immediately that he had a high fever. He was alone and his mind was wandering. He had cracked up during those hours out in the snow. His forehead had taken on the same dark-red color as that of the earth walls and his hot, dry lips hung open. The fire was still burning in the stove, and from inside the lamp came the piping or whistling sound of carbide reacting. Every time the sound intensified, he lifted his head and looked at the ceiling with wide-open eyes, at the same time gesticulating repeatedly with his black hands.

I heard my name called from the woods. It was Ledin. I hastily threw some wood into the stove and spread reindeer skins over Plennik. Suddenly I heard him say, clearly and unmistakably:

"Why are you staring at me?"

"Plennik," I said. "Take it easy now. You'll find your own people again. Or they'll find you. They're close by. We could see that today. They'll come. Wait for them. Just take it easy. The fever will run its course. But you're going to be all alone for a while. Until they come."

He did not say anything and he did not look at me.

"The rest of us are getting out of here," I continued. "Right away. We may have found a way out."

"Go," he answered, and it now seemed that he had fully regained his senses.

"What can I do for you?" I said.

"Nothing," he answered, and a great calm seemed to come over him.

"How are you going to make it alone?" I asked.

"I'm not going to make it," he answered. "You know that. I'm not going to make anything at all."

Then, to give him hope and strength, it occurred to me to say:

"Plennik, you must know that the woman — the one the Bouncer found that night in the woods — it wasn't necessarily — I mean it could have been Elisa — you can't tell them apart when they sing . . ."

He lay with his eyes shut and listened without interrupting. Then I went a little further.

"Plennik," I said eagerly. "Now listen to me. I talked about it with the Bouncer. Forced him . . ."

But Plennik opened his eyes, raised one hand, and pointed toward the stove. I twisted about in surprise and saw a small object hanging from the stovepipe—a little round piece of bread suspended in a net to thaw out in the warmth. The Bouncer had done it. The bread was of a special shape. It was Lúnnaja's bread that Plennik himself had talked about. It was the *prosphorá,* the bread of love. Half of it was yellow-red with dried blood.

I was silent with shame. Hunchbacked with lying. Then he suddenly took my hand in both of his, as if seized with fear. Ledin had called again, more impatient than before.

"Don't let him come here," he begged excitedly. "There's nothing for him to do here."

And I understood. Ledin would perhaps "free" Plennik if he came, and he would do it out of compassion.

"I want to lie here," Plennik continued in a voice lowered almost to a whisper. "I want to lie here all alone. Here it is beautiful."

I looked questioningly at him.

"Yes," he said "Here it is so beautiful."

The fever seized him again and his light eyes looked far, far away.

"I can hear her," he said. "She's singing now."

He raised his head and listened. What he heard was the whining of the carbide lamp. And to me too it sounded like a faint, distant, beautiful song.

Ledin called again. He was very close now, no more than a few steps from the hole. I sprang up and scrambled out.

Outside all had changed. Ledin's taciturn, decisive strength had whipped everything into life and motion. In the heavy grey dusk, eyes shone with hope and assurance. Eighteen men, smeared with red-brown dirt, had taken to skis, thrown their weapons on their backs, and left all else behind.

CHAPTER 17

SIGNAL

AT DAWN

It is raining outside. The faint, cold light of dawn is one with the rain. I cannot distinguish between the rain and the light. I rise from the table with the mimosa on it and walk toward the window, but stop in the middle of the

110

room. I am gripped by a vague, nervous dread that the rain will somehow keep me from leaving the room and shut me in with the old lady. Her room is certainly pretty, but it frightens me nevertheless, as if the walls were clammy with all the mortifications of a lifetime. I cannot yet distinguish any object in this room, although I seem to discern a portrait hanging on one wall straight in front of me. A portrait of a man, conceivably in middle age. I imagine that he sits there on the wall and hates me — and I hate him. Tom's simple, yet graphic description of his father comes back to me. I see this successful man who was a spiritual pedant, who heard, not the harmony of the symphony, but only the sound of felt hammers striking steel strings, air forced through constrictions, horsehair over gut.

I become impatient and sense clearly that the woman at the table wishes to be accused, as one does when one is deeply unhappy, in order to force the issue, so that one has nothing more to fear. I have to control myself to the utmost to keep from asking her if she has never known that love means something and that lovelessness is correspondingly significant. That it poisons all who grow up in its chill. That they become men who kill much around them. Who bear guilt for much evil. Who tear down. Who are "hunchbacks."

Suddenly, while I am still standing there in the middle of the room, the still, grey dawn is shattered in the same pitiless fashion as when a flare cleaves the polar night. It is a signal that transfixes both of us. A shrill, steely, heartless signal from the telephone apparatus, quickly followed by another. A long-distance signal, from far away.

The old lady starts so violently that the vase on the rickety table is knocked over, and I can hear water dripping from the tabletop down to the floor. It is as if the rain of dawn has penetrated in to us.

111

But she remains seated and cannot muster the strength to rise. From where I stand behind her, she seems to have shrunk together from some dispirited feebleness and become much smaller. She is like a fledgling, a baby bird who turned old without ever having been clad in protective feathers.

I advance to help her to the telephone. I bend over to take her in my arms and raise her up. But I bend further and further, and before I know it, I am on my knees with my head against her breast, against the black silk blouse, against the heart that I can hear beating fast and hard. My terror at the sound of that short, metallic, military signal, which makes me smell that man who was more interested in the origin of sound than in its harmony — that terror has been transmuted into infinite compassion. And I beg her humbly to ignore the ringing, not to bother to answer.

Then I feel the warmth of her hand, discreetly laid on my head. And for a brief moment I am both her sons, Tom and the Bouncer.

I want to say something to her but I cannot speak. I want to say something to the effect that all of us, often and in many ways, seek out unhappiness in order to break our hearts. I want to prove to her that the open wound is a port of entry — for something. For "eternal life." Or for "heaven." That through that portal we carry those we love the most.

But I simply grasp her hand and kiss it hard and long as if to force my thoughts, which would otherwise be incomprehensible to her, through her skin and into the blood stream to her very heart.

Then I leave her room, departing through the hall which still lies in darkness.

But during the moments between the opening and the closing of the outer door, I can hear behind me the tired, tormented, and yet courageous steps of one who, in spite of everything, advances to take a telephone call from far away.

I hurry down the steps out into the morning rain.